Trashy Behavior

Trashy Behavior

Jim Sanderson

LAMAR UNIVERSITY press

This book is a work of fiction. Names, characters, places, and incidents are products of the author's imagination. Any resemblance to actual events or locales, or to persons living or dead, is purely coincidental.

ISBN: 978-0-9850838-8-5
Library of Congress Control Number: 2013954500
Manufactured in the United States of America

Lamar University Press
Beaumont, Texas

Acknowledgments

"Bankers," *descant*, vol 51, 2012, winner of the 2012 Texas Institute of Letters Award Kay Cattarulla Award for best story by a Texan or about Texas.

"Comanchería." *Chariton Review*. 33:1 spring, 2010.

"Dee Price's Story," *The Book of Villains*. Ed. Josh Wood. Main Street Rag (Charlotte, NC), 2011.

"Divorce Laws." special commemorative issue of *Concho River Review*, Best of *Concho River Review*, Spring 2002, and *Concho River Review*, Spring 1992.

"Massage Therapy." *Texas Soundtracks*. Ed. Terry Dalrymple, Ink Brush Press, 2011.

"Playing Scared." *Mystery in the Wind*. Kernersville, NC: Second Wind Press, 2010.

"Pissed Away." *A Shared Voice*. Lamar University Press, 2013.

"Contrabandista Epistle." (a rewrite of "El Camino del Rio") Forthcoming in *New Border: Contemporary Voices from the Texas/Mexico Border*. Eds. Brandon D. Shuler, Robert Johnson, & Erika Garza-Johnson. Texas A&M University Press, 2013.

Other Books from Lamar University Press

Jean Andrews, *High Tides, Low Tides: the Story of Leroy Colombo*
Alan Berecka, *With Our Baggage*
David Bowles, *Flower, Song, Dance: Aztec and Mayan Poetry*
Jerry Bradley, *Crownfeathers and Effigies*
Robert Murry Davis, *An Academic Life*
Jeffrey DeLotto, *Voices Writ in Sand*
Mimi Ferebee, *Wildfires and Atmospheric Memories*
Ken Hada, *Margaritas and Redfish*
Michelle Hartman, *Disenchanted and Disgruntled*
Gretchen Johnson, *The Joy of Deception and Other Stories*
Lynn Hoggard, *Motherland: Stories and Poems from Louisiana*
Dominique Inge, *A Garden on the Brazos*
Tom Mack and Andrew Geyer, eds, *A Shared Voice*
Janet McCann, *The Crone at the Casino*
Erin Murphy, *Ancilla*
Dave Oliphant, *The Pilgrimage, Selected Poems: 1962-2012*
Harold Raley, *Louisiana Rogue*
Carol Coffee Reposa, *Underground Musicians*
Jan Seale, *Appearances*
Jan Seale, *The Parkinson Poems*

www.LamarUniversityPress.Org

Books by Jim Sanderson

Semi-Private Rooms
El Camino del Rio
A West Texas Soapbox
Safe Delivery
La Mordida
Nevin's History
Faded Love
Dolph's Team
Nothing to Lose
Hill Country Property

CONTENTS

"I've been around that trashy behavior all my life . . ."
—Sam the Lion, *The Last Picture Show*

Comanchería

Otto was on his belly, playing in the tall grass, shoving aside clumps to look at and feel for the permanence in rocks and dirt, when two great arms seized him and lifted him above the grass. From his position, he saw bare, brown, hairless thighs slashing through the bluestem grass. Ahead of him, running down the small rise, was his sister. And chasing her was a naked brown man with red streaks and designs on his back. His sister could not move well because the grass pulled at her skirt and her knees caught in its folds. The naked man chasing her hopped like a short-legged, crippled bird. The brown, naked man had a hatchet in his right hand. He whipped his head back to clear his long black braids out of his face. He gained on her.

Otto's sister got to the bottom of the rise and started fighting her skirt. When the brown man got into shorter grass, Otto saw that he wore a loin cloth. Otto's older sister, Gertrude, turned just in time to see the naked man's outstretched hand. Otto twisted and fought against the strong arms dragging him. He peered up at a wide face with a slanting nose and yellow and black stripes slashed across that wide face and crooked nose. The man grimaced, then grinned. Otto wriggled to free himself and to see his sister's race. But the strong arm held him tight and then another came around, and its hand held a blunt stone tomahawk. Otto saw stars, then felt himself drop. He fell through the long grass, gasped for air, choked on stalks of the bluestem. He tasted copper. He closed his eyes to stop the stars, then opened them to see stars dancing between the ground and his face. He pushed his chest above the ground, got to his knees, straightened, and saw his sister falling forward and the brown naked man pushing at her back. The brown man went quickly to his knees, and his right hand raised up, and he brought the hatched down three quick times, and each time his hatchet came down, Otto saw another spurt of blood.

The naked man who had just bashed Otto came up behind the man

1

who had just bashed his sister. He held his hands up and motioned as though he was questioning why the man had hacked Gertrude and not grabbed her. Then, four hands pulled Otto to a standing position. But he could not make his legs work, so the two sets of hands dragged him toward the two naked men. The man who had clubbed Gertrude stood straight up, smiled and whopped so loud that his bloody chest shook. The hands threw Otto to the feet of the man who had clubbed him, and then all the naked men's faces turned, and Otto saw the form of his mother running toward these naked men, whom Otto now knew were Indians. His father had told him stories about the Indios, Indians, Comanches, Penatekas, Lipans and had told him to avoid them.

The four Indians spread out in front of Otto and looked at his mother. From behind them, he saw their bowed legs, their loin cloths, their braided hair dangling in back of them. He could smell the mixture of sweat, grease, and piss on them. His mother stopped, held her hands to her mouth, and shrieked. The Indians whooped. His mother turned her back to them and ran. The four of them ran after her.

Otto pushed himself up, held his knees to keep them steady, tried to take a step. He could walk, but he wobbled. He saw his sister with the back of her head chopped away and her blonde hair clumped with her blood drying on the ground. He focused his eyes at the distance and saw his mother tearing her skirt to give her legs more room, so she could out run the Indians.

Otto felt a slight tremble, heard snorting, turned to see a horse jerk to a stop behind him. A man swung off the horse. The man was a black man with hair like bottlebrushes sticking out from underneath the floppy hat he had pressed on his head. He wore a dirty gray shirt, buckskin britches, and knee-high moccasins. "Stupid savages. Getting off their horses," he said. "Don't you be running and making me chase you. For some reason they want you." He looked off at the distance and chuckled. "So now they gonna try and catch that other woman, like a game of chase. If they'd stayed on they horses they'd be tomahawking her or fucking her..." He looked at Otto. "That your momma?" He spoke the American language, but not like Otto's father spoke it, or the Texans who lived close by spoke it. Otto nodded his head. "Sorry," the black man said. Otto and the black man turned to watch the Indians chase his mother. She had also managed to slip out of her shoes; barefooted, she was getting farther ahead of them. "Them's Nokoni Comanche, not Penateka's. They didn't make no treaties with you squareheads. But they sure as hell are slow creatures on foot." Otto tried to scoot away from the black man dressed in buckskins. "Don't make me chase you."

Otto stood stone still.

The black man stepped toward Otto, grabbed Otto's chin, and tilted his head. "You got at knot. Don't it hurt?"

Otto wasn't sure he knew how to speak American the way this man spoke it, or if he did speak, Otto wasn't sure that this man could understand the way Otto spoke American. He looked at the man and nodded then looked over his shoulder to see that the Comanches were gaining on his mother but that she was nearing a clump of cedar. The black man stepped closer to Gertrude and peered down. "Who's this laying over here with brains oozing out?" Otto shuddered. "What's wrong with you boy? Why ain't you crying?"

Otto's mother was getting closer to the clump of cedar. A gun shot rung out from behind the cedar, and one of the Comanches clawed at his chest. The other three stopped to look at him. When the Indian who had been shot crumpled, the other three grabbed him by either arm and a leg and began running away from the clump of cedar. Stepping out from the cedar, trying to aim a pistol with one hand, his Deutschland-made shotgun in the other, Otto's father shot twice, hitting nothing. The Comanches pulled their friend back up the rise toward Otto and the black man. Otto wanted to shout, "Papa, Papa," but no words came out of his mouth. Papa looked up and saw Otto, and Otto dimly heard Papa shout his name, "Otto."

"We ain't waiting for them savages," the black man said and pulled Otto to his standing horse. As Otto tried to say something in some way of talking, the black man pushed Otto onto the saddle and then jumped up behind him. With one arm around Otto and another arm squeezing the reins, the black man made the horse jump and run. The tips of several cedar trees raked across Otto's cheek, but the horse cleared the cedar brakes and churned through the high grass.

Otto lost sight of any of his personal landmarks or of the ones his father told him about. He knew that he was bouncing west on the back of this horse being steered by this black man. He was bad with words, but he could remember the ground, the rocks, the grass, and the trees he saw. And he tried to remember them so that he could come back to help Papa.

The Indians, Comanches, Nokoni, whatever they were, caught up with Otto and the black man. They rode smaller horses with two curved hooks for saddles on their backs and handprints and other painted designs on their haunches and shoulders. The man who had been shot tried to hold on to a horse, and when he fell, none of his friends went back to get him.

Then more Comanches joined them on like small horses, but they led or chased other horses, and one group had two girls with them. Otto recognized them. They were the Metzger girls. The older one, Ida, was two years older than Otto, the younger one, Emma, was four years younger than Otto. Their faces, outlined by their golden hair, were blank and white and covered with bruises. Their dresses were torn from getting caught on shrubs, mesquite, and cedar. In fact, Ida had both of her sleeves ripped off and red, bleeding scratches on her white arms.

They rode by moonlight late into the night. Then they camped in a creek bed and posted scouts on the edge of the slopes. As the night got later, Otto figured that they meant for him to sleep on rocks. And the Comanche who had first grabbed him tied a strip of rawhide around his leg and then stretched the rawhide out. Another Comanche held the younger Metzger daughter by her hand and pulled the older Metzger daughter by her golden hair. Otto's Comanche tied the rawhide rope to Emma's ankle, and her eyes tried to talk to Otto.

The Metzger girls' Comanche tied a rawhide thong around Ida's hands. After some time, with no light but the stars, the Comanche who held the rawhide thong tied to Ida's hands dragged her into the dark. At first she said nothing, but then she started screaming, and other Comanches followed her screaming into the dark. Otto wished that she would stop screaming. Soon she did.

They started no fires, but the Comanche who grabbed Otto and clubbed him gave Otto some dried meat and something that looked like a cake that couldn't stay together. The Indian squatted in front of Otto and smiled. The yellow and black stripes were smeared; his eyes looked small and deep in his head behind his slanted nose; so he didn't look so fierce.

He said something that came from deep down in his throat and sounded like the Deutsch that Otto spoke when he was a small child. Those words came back to Otto.

"Ich bien—" Otto said and then his mind got rattled. He tried to sort it out. It had been a long time since he had tried to use these words. "Du bist das indio," Otto said. The Comanche smiled and urged with his hands for Otto to make more words.

The Comanche looked around at his friends and smiled, but only the black man smiled back. No one else noticed. The black man stepped closer. And Otto's Comanche spoke more words that sounded like the words Otto and his family spoke when they crossed the ocean and came to Texas. But then his father stopped speaking the Deutsch words and started speaking the Texan way and said Otto should only speak the Texan too because they were no longer Deutschlanders but Texans. The Comanche spoke too rapidly for Otto to concentrate on the words. Then the Comanche motioned with his hands, waving his fingers toward Otto's chest, for Otto to speak.

"Yo soy un Texicano," Otto said.

"Sí," the Comanche said and urged Otto to say more. Otto felt a tug on his ankle, turned to see Emma staring blanked faced at him. His smile made her smile, and she scooted closer to Otto. Otto's Comanche pulled Otto's chin away from Emma and back to him. He spoke the language that the Mexicans spoke. Otto tried to listen but got confused.

All his life, as the words he heard and tried to use changed, Otto listened as close as he could and watched as hard as he could as people used their sets of words. Each set of words made their speakers make different faces. The words came out with different sounds attached to them. The words, Otto knew, meant things. But with the way the different sets of words made their speakers' faces, mouths, and sounds change, Otto wasn't sure that the words couldn't change the things. So he distrusted words. When this Comanche grabbed him, Otto was looking at the permanence of things: the grass, the dirt, the sky. He shook his head. The Indian slapped him, smiled, then walked away.

The black man sat beside Otto stretched out. "You better eat what he give you."

Otto tried to bite into the meat, couldn't, then tried the cake. It tasted like uncooked oatmeal.

"Tonkawas call it Pemmican. It's squished and dried berries and nuts and the like," the black man said. As Otto sat and tried to chew his meal, the black man sat across from him. "You decide you gonna talk?"

Otto looked at him, afraid once again, to talk. "I like a little conversation from somebody other than these Comanches. So if you don't talk, it's gonna be a one-sided conversation."

"Nothing to say," Otto found himself saying.

"Well, that's good, that's just fine. You already said more words to me than you said to Grinning Badger there." He motioned his head toward Otto's Comanche. "Badger there thinks he's got some powerful medicine, some kind of dried Mexican pestle or something like that, so he's leading this here raiding party. He's thinking they're all safe, till the one you seen got hisself shot chasing that woman I figure was your mama." Otto found himself nodding. "Well, you done real good so far. Ol' Badger there, he Nokoni, hears from Penatekas about the white people who speak some kind of strange Comanche. So he wants to hear 'em. Course he wants to steal from 'em and kill a few too. So now, he's talked to you. You lucky. I got no idea why you're alive. He either wants you as a slave or wants to trade you as a slave to Comancheros out of Las Vegas. Hell, you lucky he ain't gelded you. Hell, I'm lucky I ain't gelded and a proper slave. Boy, could you motion your head just so I know you concentrating?"

Otto nodded, and he felt Emma pull up close to him and put her hand on his thigh.

The black man touched Otto's cheek.

He turned his face from the black man to Emma, then back again. "You listening?"

Otto nodded.

"My name is Thomas Jefferson Monroe. Of course that ain't my real name, but I figure if Indians can choose a name, I can choose a name. So I chose."

"Otto," Otto said.

"So you Otto? Now, see, we talking."

Otto nodded. Emma snuggled up to him, curled around herself like a dog does, and went fast to sleep. Otto tried not to breathe.

"Otto, you ever hear of the black Seminoles?" While Thomas Jefferson Moore talked, Otto watched sleeping Emma. "I'm one. I escaped my Georgia master and run to Florida and joined the Seminole Indians. Problem was they made me a slave too. So I hunted and roamed and raided with them. I saved me some goods and bought my freedom. Now I'm here. All the good it's done me. Come with a whole bunch of other black Seminoles. Went down to Mexico, but times was tough. So I'm riding around with these savages trying to trade with them. I ain't sure why they tolerate me."

Otto could not keep track of what Thomas Jefferson Monroe had told him: the changing of a name, the new tribe—Seminoles, Mexico, Comanches. He wrapped his arm around Emma.

Otto didn't remember Deutschland, but he remembered coming to Texas, a new country, and then to a place called Braunfels and then Fredericksburg, and then to a new house in the Loyal Valley. He dimly remembered being hungry most of the journey and his father telling him that he would have food if they could all be Texans. And before they got to the Loyal valley, Mama got sick, and Heinrich, a older brother died, and Gertrude almost died—all of a sickness that made everything in their bodies turn to smelly gush and come out their mouths and arses.

When they got better, Papa said they were not Texans but part of a United States and were Americans. And Otto saw Mexicans, and Papa said that Texans used to be Mexicans before they became Texans and then Americans. And now some Texans no longer wanted Texas to be a state in the United States but wanted to become Texans again and not Americans. The problems were the words. They changed over and over. And if people kept changing the words, then the things that the words meant may change as well.

Otto woke up when some Comanches dragged Ida back. She looked directly at Otto and tried to make words. But she had a gag over her mouth, and her skirt was torn away. Otto did not wake Emma.

Otto knew Emma and Ida from the school that he went to. They were good at school, but because he was no good with words, he was no good at school. But now that school was out, he had been trying to help his father. But he was also no good at herding the cattle or tending the corn or the peach orchards that his father had been tending for several years.

* * *

The next morning, the Comanches put Otto on a horse and then put Emma behind him on the same horse. Thomas Jefferson Monroe held the reins to their horse. Next to them, Ida had a horse of her own. The two sisters stared at each other and seemed be saying things without words. Thomas Jefferson said words, "Now you two children hang on. You jump off this horse, you gonna kill yourself or get clubbed for trying." But before they could start, Ida grabbed at the reins of her horse, got them from the Comanche, and kicked the horse. The horse spun, and as it did, Emma jumped off from behind Otto and ran to her sister and the screaming horse. Emma jumped and grabbed the horse's mane and her sister's dress, and then the horse pushed on, away from the others and up the rocky ravine.

Otto looked at Thomas Jefferson, who grasped the reins tightly, "Don't you do it, boy." But Otto jumped off the horse, hopped and jumped up the ravine. The Comanches rode past him, on their way to the sisters. Otto had to dodge some of them. He cleared the ravine, his feet rolling on the rocks and weeds, his chest hurting from sucking in air, his thighs burning from the running, the horse with Ida mounted and Emma hanging on getting smaller in the distance. He knew that he could not close that distance, but he kept running, the Comanches still riding past him toward the girls. But through his sweat, he saw Emma fall. She stayed down for a moment, but then darted on.

The Comanches kept after Ida, so Otto tried to catch Emma. She skirted away from her sister and looked over her shoulder to see who was chasing her. Otto checked too. Only he was chasing her. He seemed to run easily, and he closed in on her, and then she and he scooted down another rocky slope on their palms, butts, and soles of their shoes. Before she reached the bottom of the slope, Emma tried to stand, but she couldn't and tumbled head first into more rocks and gravel and went into a roll. Otto did make it to his feet, and he caught Emma. But once he caught up to her, he put his hands on his knees, bent over in front of her, and sucked hard for air. Emma had an egg-sized knot on her forehead and blood was coming out of her nose. Her wide-eyed look told Otto that she wanted to say something, wanted to tell him something, but she could not make words. Otto said, "Hide."

Emma looked, ran quickly to the exposed roots of an oak, and squeezed her body in between the roots. Otto ran to her. From the dark space, she looked out at Otto then pushed herself through rock and mud deeper into her tiny cave. Otto looked around him, then started stacking rocks around the opening between the roots. He stepped back to see that Emma was entombed, and then he ran forward to catch Ida, the Comanches, or Thomas Jefferson.

Otto heard hollow thuds from behind him: hooves on rocks. He kept running but was swept up, again by strong brown arms, and as his feet left the ground, this time he twisted, squirmed, and fought the force of the arms. The Comanche dropped him on his knees, and he winced from the pain shooting up his thighs. The Comanche was off his horse, so Otto was in a foot race. Though his knees were sore, Otto ran, and he put distance between himself and the Comanche, and he put even more distance between the Comanche and Emma. When the Comanche realized that Otto was running back the same direction he had just come, the Comanche turned his back to Otto, went back to his horse, and let Otto run on. Running was just what Otto did. When he ran, his feet hit the ground; he was close to the ground; he could see the ground beneath him, just as he could when the brown arms seized him. On a horse, he was too far away from the ground. He ran into and out of a ravine, then down another one to the place that he had just run from, to the camp that the Comanches were leaving.

He found Thomas Jefferson sitting cross-legged, smoking a pipe, with his horse behind him, tied to a tree. "My, my, ain't you a mess. You got yourself in all kinds of trouble. I'm gonna miss you," Thomas Jefferson said. Otto sat down beside Thomas Jefferson. Across from Thomas Jefferson, under a tree, his head in his hands, his eyes sad, sat Grinning Badger. Grinning Badger held out his hands as though to ask why Otto had returned. They all waited.

The Comanches came back, and the man who had led Ida into the dark the night before rode behind her on the horse she had led away. Her face was black and blue; she had bleeding gashes in her arms. She whimpered. The other Comanches filed into camp. None of them had Emma. Grinning Badger stayed where he was and watched the Comanche with Ida. That Comanche shoved her off her horse and was just as quickly behind her. He pulled at her dress until it ripped off her. Then with his knife, from behind her, he slit her undergarments and pulled them off to expose her naked chest. He reached in front of her, knife in hand, and in one move sliced off her right breast and flung the lump of tissue and fat onto the rocks.

Ida looked, with the rest of the Comanches, at the round pink, raw, bloody spot that had been her breast. She pulled her head up. The Comanches looked at her. Then she began to scream. She didn't make words, just deep, loud sounds like an animal caught in a trap. Otto looked at the Comanches; they looked at each other. The continual screaming spooked them all. So the Comanche who had just sliced off her breast, pulled her hair back, then pulled his knife across her throat. Blood spurted, and then Ida crumpled at the Comanche's feet.

All the Comanche eyes were on Otto. Then, Grinnng Badger rose and motioned with his hands as though questioning the man who had just killed Ida. Looking grieved and upset, he walked slowly toward Otto. Thomas Jefferson scooted away. When Grinning Badger got close, he grabbed Otto's right hand, squeezed all of his knuckles into a balled fist, leaving only Otto's pointing finger sticking from his fist. Then, he pulled Otto over and down until he had Otto's finger resting on a flat rock. And just as quickly as his friend had mutilated Ida, Grinning Badger hacked off Otto's finger. Otto looked at his dismembered finger, then at Grinning Badger's tortured eyes.

Grinning Badger yelled some words, moved away from Otto, and the Comanches started mounting their horses. Otto tried to move his finger and watched it lie still and bloody in front of him. Thomas Jefferson said from behind him, "You lucky it was your finger, boy."

The next night, they camped on a hill, and they could see in front of them the land growing ragged and flat without trees. Otto again chewed the pemmican and looked at his right hand. From the light of the full moon, he could see his finger, and with his left, he gingerly touched the mud and herb poultice that Thomas Jefferson had wrapped it in. It throbbed still. And he knew that he has thrown up and lost his senses as Thomas Jefferson led his horse. Eventually Thomas Jefferson had tied his hands around the horses neck so he wouldn't fall off.

As Otto chewed and felt both hungry and sick, Thomas Jefferson talked. "I saved your finger, and looky here." He held up Otto's finger by a rawhide string that he had poked through the middle joint of the finger. "This is gonna make you a nice trinket. You can wear it around your neck. Who knows? It could become powerful medicine." Otto said nothing. "Here boy," he hung the finger around Otto's neck. "I poked that rawhide string clear through the bone. It rots, you gonna have a nice boney finger for jewelry."

Otto looked down at the bloody flesh that had been his finger dangling below his chin. Thomas Jefferson said, "You lucky to be alive." Thomas Jefferson then reached to Otto's head to feel his forehead. "You ain't got a fever."

"See, Comanches ain't their real names. They call themselves Nermernuh. That means people. So you see, to the Nermernuh, you may look like a human being, but you ain't. You just an animal looks human." Thomas Jefferson leaned away from him. "Course, they wouldn't treat most animals like they done that gold-haired girl. They got this mean streak."

Otto pointed at Grinning Badger, then asked, "Is he good people?"

"You talking again? How many times is that in one day?" Thomas Jefferson asked, then studied Grinning Badger, "Now Grinning Badger, I think he wants young folks for slaves or for children. Ten or so years ago, they was hit real bad with the fevers. Lots of Nokoni died. They need more people to hold on to their Comanchería."

His Papa had told him that they were from good people in Deutschland, not the aristocracy, but just beneath them. His Papa said the Texans would not know this. But be that as it may, Papa said that his family and the other Deutschalnders should show the Texans that they were good people. And sooner or later the Texans would know. Otto was wondering if the Comanches knew or could know if he was from the good people. And then he wondered if he had failed to show them.

* * *

Now the lone captive or slave, Otto and the Comanches rode out into the flat brown land without many trees. The throb in his finger kept time with the pounding of his heart. And the hotness that pushed down on them from way up in the sky made the throb sound in Otto's ears and made the skin stretch even tighter. The Comanches slowed their pace. They seemed to have relaxed and gotten into a better mood. Some pulled their arms back to expose their naked chests to the sun and absorb the heat. They smiled or poked each other. Thomas Jefferson riding alongside Otto explained, "Comanche always like plains country the real Comanchería. Comanche is a horse people, not like the Seminole. Comanche likes it best when he can sit his horse and see a long distance. Makes him feel he's got good medicine just being him." Sometimes, during the march, young men would have their own races, or run figure eight on the ponies. And sometimes, the all of them would admire and pamper their captured horses."

They camped in some short stumpy trees along a riverbed. Beneath them a river struggled toward the hills they had come from. This night, they had a fire and strips of venison from a deer that they killed. They joked and ate and wrestled and smiled and generally left Otto alone. Late, as most had rolled over to go to sleep, Thomas Jefferson held Otto's hand up to the light from the fire. He squeezed the stump, and Otto breathed in to keep from screaming because he saw what had happened to Emma when she screamed. "It's hot to the touch and hurting you. It's festering."

Grinning Badger stepped out of the darkness and into the light of the fire. He looked down at kneeling Otto, squatted in front of him, and took Otto's hand from Thomas Jefferson. He jerked the hand one way, then the other and looked cross ways over his slanted nose at the finger. He raised his long sharp knife over the hand, pushed out Otto's stump, then pulled his knife along the flesh of the stump. Otto's finger did not hurt, and he watched the yellowish, green pus ooze out of the slice in the finger. Thomas Jefferson nodded, wrapped a handkerchief around the nub, then caked it in another poultice. "It's bad now, but it's gonna heal. Better, I think he likes you. You must of somehow impressed with all you done You may end up living with him instead being his slave. What you got to say about that?"

Otto said nothing. "That's what I figured. You got nothing to say about nothing. Watching your loved ones get hacked up and all you do is stare at me with them big eyes. A man like myself likes talking, so I end up trying to get words out of you."

Otto concentrated. "I want with you."

"Well look, you is talking again."

Otto looked back toward Grinning Badger and shook his head. Then he pointed to Thomas Jefferson. "You can't come with me. I travel amongst them. I got no home."

Otto put his thumb to his chest, nodded, and said, "No home too."

"Grinning Badger is powerful." Otto shook his head. "You going to get yourself killed," he said to Otto. "This ain't no argument. I ain't rescuing you from no Comanches and get myself carved up." He turned his back to Otto. But after a few moments, he swivelled back to face Otto. "So what could you give me if I take you back to your folks? What would your folks give me?"

"I stay with you," Otto said and felt himself smile.

"Ain't that the damndest. Well, you can't. I'd think you'd want to get some sleep after stuffing yourself with that meat." Thomas Jefferson spread himself along the ground and was soon asleep.

The next day they marched along the river bank until it flattened out, and the river spread out over the flat grass and dirt. And here with the wide, shallow water was a small Comanche camp. The Comanches in the party raced their captured ponies through and around the tipis of the village, and then they all returned to the center of the village, next to the river. Still mounted, the returning raiders whooped, words or sounds, and the words or sounds encouraged other words or sounds, and soon the whole village was screeching and dancing in place. Then they jumped off their horses, and women ran to the men and hugged the men, and the whole time no one stopped shaking, screaming, or writhing. Otto watched all of this from atop his horse. He could see that it was a celebration by people who understood each other without words. And then an old woman pulled Otto off his horse, smiled at him, and then began to beat him with a switch. Suddenly there were other women around him, and they all began to beat him with switches.

Otto looked around him for Thomas Jefferson and saw him step closer, but then the women turned toward Thomas Jefferson and whipped him with switches until he left Otto to them. Otto then reached to his chest and under his shirt and pulled up his bloody finger. One old lady tried to grab his magic, but Otto folded his fist over the finger and clutched it. His feet gave way, and they still beat him, and some kicked him. Even girls ran to him and got in on the fun. A few fetched coals from a fire with wooden or horn spoons and dropped the coals on Otto. He writhed but held on to his finger.

One face in particular caught Otto's attention. It belonged to another blonde child, a girl, about as old as Otto, and where she should have had a nose she had a black, singed, raw hole. She stared while the others whipped. His mind lost track of where he was or how much time had passed, but by sundown the women had left him on the ground. His hands and feet were tied, and he had a leash around his neck, and the other end was staked into the ground. He looked around as best he could and saw the blonde girl with the burned off nose. "Du bist einen jugend Deütschlander?"

"Yes, ja, sí."

She smiled, said something that was the Comanche Deutsch. Otto tried to unscramble his tongue, to come with some words. She hesitantly stepped toward Otto, knelt, and Otto gazed at the hole in her face. She tilted her head, and Otto tilted his gaze toward the hole. She reached for the rawhide around Otto's wrist, then she grabbed the thongs and delicately began to unravel the knots in them. With her face close to his, Otto could hear the whistling of her breathing. Then, they both heard footsteps, and like a small bird, she skittered off. "They burned her nose off with coals or hot sticks," Otto heard from behind him, then twisted to see Thomas Jefferson standing above him. "You poor child." Thomas Jefferson knelt. "But I dast not set you free. I dast not." Otto could see his own reflection in Thomas Jefferson's eyes. "You try to fight them women. Show them you got strong medicine," Thomas Jefferson said. Then he straightened up. Thomas Jefferson checked once back over his shoulder as he left Otto.

Otto spent the night pulling against the rawhide bindings on his wrists, but if he pulled too tightly against his leash, it choked him. He wore himself out and then went to sleep. At sunrise, Grinning Badger came to him and cut him lose. He gave an order in words that Otto could now recognize as Comanche. He turned and walked away, and Otto figured that Grinning Badger's words must have meant for Otto to follow him.

14

Otto followed him through the camp, through the early morning coolness, through the smoke of morning fires, through the smells that came from humans pressed too close together. When Grinning Badger ducked into a tipi, Otto followed him.

In the tent was a woman with an infant at her breast and a boy several years younger than Otto. Grinning Badger pointed to one side of the woman and said Comanche words, which Otto took to mean to sit. So he sat where Grinning Badger pointed. Then Grinning Badger ducked back outside of the tent. The young boy crawled over his mother's lap and his brother sucking down breakfast and sat by Otto. He reached out and touched the whelps on Otto's face. Then gingerly, he reached for the finger dangling around Otto's chest. He poked it, withdrew his hand, and then Otto grabbed his finger between two whole ones and held it up for the boy to see. The boy chuckled, then grabbed the finger himself. He pointed it at Otto and then shook it at him as though scolding him for losing his finger.

Grinning Badger ducked back into the tent, and the girl with the burned nose followed him in. Grinning Badger kicked at her and smiled, but she dodged him and huddled away from the others. In Grinning Badger's hands were strips of hot, steaming, greasy meat. He passed them out. And everybody, Otto included, clawed and chewed the meat. Then Grinning Badger came back with his hands full of long white tubes. He passed these out, and the girl with no nose and the boy sucked on the tubes, and then tore at the tubes with their teeth. Even though he figured out that these tubes were like the casings for his papa's sausage, Otto ate the intestines. He warily watched Grinning Badger. Without the black and yellow slashes, the face looked normal and unimposing, so Otto relaxed and pulled the intestines with his teeth.

"We belong to him," the girl with no nose said and pointed to Grinning Badger. "He wants jüngen." Grinning badger looked sternly at her, and she went back to eating her intestines.

After his meal, the others left the tipi, but Otto went back to sleep, woke up, went back to sleep, ate again, slept through the night, woke the next morning, and ventured out from the tipi. He wandered around, and no women beat him, no men tied him up. He eventually found some other boys his age. They all tried to touch his finger. He let them, and they did not try to take it away. He watched them as they made arrows, rode

15

horses, and then shot the arrows. When they started racing on foot, he joined them. Though his welts hurt and his limbs were all sore, Otto found that he could outrun all of them. He beat them over and over again. Like their fathers, they hopped like crippled birds rather than really running. Then he traded his shoes for one of the boys' moccasins. And without his thick-soled shoes, he was even faster. As always, he wanted the ground beneath him, under his feet. He grew confident that, as long as could feel the ground, knew it was there, he could move quickly across it.

By the end of the day, his finger had started attracting files, so he took if from around his neck and stuffed it in his pocket. And later still, Thomas Jefferson showed up. He and Thomas Jefferson walked to the edge of the water and sat in the mud and dangled their feet in the water. Otto noticed that Thomas Jefferson now had the start of a beard. Thomas Jefferson slapped Otto on the back, took off his drooping, wide-brimmed hat, laid it on the dry land, pushed himself up, and waded into the water, then he lay in the water and sloshed it on him. "Don't you need a bath?" he asked.

Otto joined him and lay in the water and felt the slight current pulling at his shirt and pants. He remembered his finger, and washed the dried blood off of it in the river. "Old Grinning Badger must like you or had pity on you. You could become a part of this tribe, not a slave. You already in Comanchería, but Grinning Badger might take you into the heart of it and show you the Llano Estacado. You might see the Comancheros over in Las Vegas or get see Cheyenne or kill a Ute. Who knows? Ain't nothing freer than a Comanche on a horse in the Comanchería. Ain't nothing but you. But now you earn your keep around here and try to become just like them and listen to Grinning Badger. Don't worry about no freedom."

"What words do I say?"

"Looky there, you almost talking regular," Thomas Jefferson said. "They mostly talk Comanche. So you best learn some of their words."

Otto didn't know if he could learn some more words. "I can't."

"It ain't so hard. I talk Spanish, American, Comanche, and a little Cherokee, Apache, and Tonkawa. You just got to listen."

"I try to listen, but there is too many words."

"Well then, you listen better. Tomorrow, I'm leaving. I got business with my own."

"I go with you," Otto said.

"No you don't go with me. You're better off here now that Grinning Badger's looking after you. So you got to try to understand. You ain't gonna have me to explain things to you. And I got business. A man of my stature and knowledge can make some money with these savages. But you, you might see all the Comanchería." Otto didn't know if he could understand without Thomas Jefferson. As far as Otto was concerned, he understood Thomas Jefferson better than he understood his papa.

* * *

The next morning, Otto was awakened by movement. He forced himself out of that dull existence between sleep and wakefulness to see Grinning Badger's wife pressing her baby into her shoulder and his son running around the tipi. When he listened, he heard popping sounds coming from a distance. Grinning Badger came into the tipi, grabbed the boy in his arms, and pulled his wife by the wrist to the opening of the tipi. He pushed them outside and turned to stare at Otto. His gaze stopped Otto, and Otto thought that maybe he was about to be beaten or about to lose another finger. But Grinning Badger left Otto alone in the tipi.

Otto sat, heard more popping sounds, heard screaming, heard the crackling of fire, then saw tiny orange specks on the tipi. The orange spots grew larger, then flared, and shards of burning leather fell in on Otto. He clutched his finger around his neck, waited, smelled the burning leather, and darted out of the tipi into screaming, running, and shooting.

Comanche men, women, and children were running in wild patterns throughout the village. Some of the old women who had beaten him held their hands above their heads while they ran. Men tried to string bows or aim a rifle or pistol. Then Otto saw the cause. A woman's face exploded into a bloody mist, and behind her was an American solider in a blue shirt aiming his pistol.

Otto stepped into the running Comanches, ran with some of them, not trying to pass any of them. Blue-uniformed American horsemen darted in amongst them and fired into them. Some Comanches fired a gun or arrow over the heads of their families at the soldiers. One of the mounted

Comanches was Grinning Badger, so Otto ran toward him. A mounted soldier was in front of him. "You, you're white," he heard and kept running toward Grinning Badger. "Stop, boy," the soldier yelled after him.

When Otto got close to Grinning Badger, Grinning Badger scowled at him and screamed at the attackers. He pulled his horse around by the reins, dug his heels into the horse's flanks, and raced through the crowd. Two mounted soldiers followed. Otto, on foot, tried to follow.

Running, dodging people, his feet slapping the ground, Otto watched as Grinning Badger cleared the village. A mounted soldier passed him, then another, and a third. He saw the four silhouettes in front of him moving out of the village and up a slight incline. Otto noticed that he was leaving the village behind him. Grinning Badger, he realized, was leading as many of the attackers away as he could.

He saw the soldiers aim and then heard them fire. He saw a faint red mist dabble Grinning Badger's back and his horse's haunches. Grinning Badger's figure grew smaller as it gained distance, but Otto saw the horse stumble, the soldiers gain on him. Grinning Badger was off his horse and running. He ran up the incline toward a bare, dying tree, pressed his back against a fork in the tree's trunk, and waited.

Otto got closer and closer. He saw the soldiers rein up their horses, dismount, and stare at Grinning Badger. As he got closer yet, he saw Grinning Badger's chest heaving, saw him raise his head to look at the soldiers. Otto saw the three soldiers aim. Their guns popped and smoked in unison.

Otto's lungs burned; his legs were beyond pain and began to feel hollow. He pulled himself up the incline. As he ran past the soldiers, Grinning Badger looked at him, and Otto tried to memorize the face with the slanted nose with no black and yellow stripes, the totally normal face. Grinning Badger slumped, his chest and head falling forward, but the tree kept him standing. As Otto got closer, the weight of Grinning Badger's sagging head and torso pulled him forward, and he fell face first onto the hard ground. Otto moved closer, but just as he was about to touch Grinning Badger, two soldiers grabbed him from behind and held him tightly.

The soldiers mounted, and one of them pulled Otto behind him on his horse. Then they rode back to the village. As they rode through it from the other side, Otto looked over the soldier's shoulder too see other American soldiers in the gaudy blue shirts and dirty tan pants dragging Comanche bodies into piles. In the distance were a line of people, the survivors trudging off into the flat tan wilderness. When they cleared the village, the soldiers halted in front of an American soldier and a small Texan with a tobacco stained beard. The soldier steering the horse lowered Otto onto the ground.

"We ought to go get the rest," the small Texan said.

"Let them be," the American soldier said. "We've killed enough."

"The point is to kill 'em all."

"No need to risk anymore of our own lives."

Other soldiers began leading captives to the American solider giving the orders and the small Texan with the tobacco stained beard. They were mostly women and children. They brought forth the girl with the burned off nose. "Oh Jesus," the small Texan said. "Hell Lieutenant, I say we go kill some more of em."

"Mr. Jumpers, please," the American solider said.

"Well then why don't you just kill that poor little girl? What chance is she going have back in civilization?"

The Lieutenant pulled off his wide-brimmed hat and slapped it on his thigh. "Mr. Jumpers, from the very start, from the point we let you join us, I made it absolutely clear that, if we were to continue, we would follow federal policy."

"Thanks for your goddamn help. Course it was me suggested we abandon the trail and light for the upper Concho, Ranger style." Then Jumpers looked at Otto. "I bet he's the German boy." Both the Lieutenant and Jumpers stepped toward Otto, but they halted when they heard powerful, loud cursing. Two soldiers dragged a tied, screaming, cursing Thomas Jefferson to them. "Now he's mine," the small Texan said and pointed to Thomas Jefferson. "I'm the one found him and claimed him. I'm the one gonna take him to Bastrop and sell him. He's mine. You federalists back off."

"This is a quandary," the Lieutenant said and put his slouch hat back on. "He's an enemy captive."

"He's a nigger worth $800, and he's mine," Jumpers said. "It'd be a hell of thing not to get some profit after all the trouble these savages put us through." The soldier behind Otto nodded.

"We'll take him to Fort Mason, and we'll see what the commandant says."

"He's property," Jumpers said.

"And, unlike most of my fellow officers, I'm a free-stater, so you just wait."

Thomas Jefferson's wrists were tied, but he pulled his shoulder away from the soldiers who tried to hold him. "You might as well kill me now cause you ain't gonna make me no slave nor no prisoner. I done been both and ain't going back." The soldiers all grabbed Thomas Jefferson and pushed him to his knees, then wrestled him to the ground. Between the arms and knees of the soldiers, he looked at Otto. "You tell them Otto. I ain't no Comanche, but I ain't no nigger slave neither. I'm a businessman."

Otto tried to sum up what he knew of Thomas Jefferson and tried to put those thoughts and memories into words. Jumpers, the lieutenant, Thomas Jefferson, and the little girl without the nose looked at him and waited for his words. "Du verstehst," Otto said to Thomas Jefferson.

"In English, Otto," Otto heard from behind him. Otto whirled around. Pale-faced, red-eyed, powder and sun burned, his moustache untrimmed, his Deutschland crafted shotgun cradled in his arm stood Papa. "You must talk English for them to understand," Papa said.

"Otto," Thomas Jefferson yelled. "You tell them 'bout me."

But Otto stepped to his father who held out his arms. "Your Mama is good. Your sister was... was... killed by the savages." Otto hugged his crying father, then stepped back, pulled his decaying finger out of his pocket, and showed it to his father.

* * *

As they started back, even that day, after putting fire to the bodies and leaving them burning, Otto, riding beside his father near the head of a long column of soldiers and their captives, tried to listen, tried to talk, tried to order his memories. He heard his father tell him that the Deutschlanders in the Loyal Valley met with the ex-Texas Ranger Jumpers, and rode to Fort Mason and begged for federal help. There was no help at the fort, but the commander told them about a patrol under

Lieutenant Bartlett. Only Jumpers and Papa went on, they met Bartlett, and at Jumper's insistence, they headed toward the upper Concho, gambling that Grinning Badger and his band would be camped somewhere along it.

As Papa waited for Otto's story, Otto's mind froze on one memory. But he needed words. He only had one, "Emma!"

"Was ist los?" Papa said, then corrected himself. "What has happened? Otto, where is she?" Then Papa yelled, "Wait," to Lieutenant Bartlett riding alone at the head of the column. Bartlett held up his hand, and soldiers pulled their horses up around Otto. "The Metzger girl. Otto knows where the other Metzger girl is," Papa said.

Jumpers pulled his horse up. Tied to the horn of his Texas saddle were the reins to Thomas Jefferson's horse. "Where is she, Otto?" Papa asked again.

Otto tried to duck from the eyes that were on him. "She is in a nest, in a tree."

"I can get you there," Thomas Jefferson said. "If you let me go."

Jumpers pulled out a pistol and pointed it at Thomas Jefferson's head. "You get us there, or I'll give up my $800 and put a bullet through your head." Thomas Jefferson, Papa, and Otto all looked at Bartlett for help, but Bartlett said nothing.

So the column followed tied-up Thomas Jefferson. Otto noted the trees, the ground, the rocks that looked familiar. He could remember them and distinguish them better than he could words. And he felt, for all his welts and bruises and missing finger, he had had a small triumph. He was not lost. He knew where he was and how to get back to Loyal Valley or how to get back to the smoldering Comanche village. He could probably lead them as well as Thomas Jefferson especially if he were on foot.

They camped for the night, and Otto slept by his father, but when everyone was asleep, Otto crept to the little girl with no nose. She woke from his staring at her. "What kind of words can you talk?" he asked her.

"I can talk the English," she said.

"I have trouble with words."

"Me, too," she said with the whistling sound that the air made through her nose.

Otto motioned with his hands and said, "Why did you try to take the ties off my hands?"

"I don't like people be tied," she said.

"Otto," Otto said and pointed to himself.

The girl with no nose said a Comanche word. But then she said, "Smells" and pointed to herself. "Comanche name."

Otto touched his finger to his nose. He couldn't see well in the moonlight, but she gingerly reached for the rough hole in her face. Otto waited for an answer. "The women did it," she said. Then she wouldn't look at Otto.

He walked through the camp and was spotted by one of the American soldiers, but the soldier let him go on. He went to Thomas Jefferson. He pushed Thomas Jefferson's shoulder until he woke him. When Thomas Jefferson recognized him, he begged, "Help me, boy."

"Emma," Otto said.

"Okay, tomorrow we find Emma. Then you gonna help me, boy." Otto nodded.

The next afternoon, Otto knew that he could have found the creek where he and Emma had hid from the Comanches. The soldiers discovered Ida's corpse. Papa, haggard and stooped-shouldered, demanded that they scoop up the remains and take her back to her people. Jumpers said that was stupid, that she was stinking already. Lieutenant Bartlett said that he would have some men bury the body where it was.

Then Otto led them to Emma. He found her, skinny, covered with insect bites and cuts, sitting by a tree eating unripe pecans, acorns, and roots. She had gotten sick and vomited. But she had eaten. She smiled but said nothing. She pointed at Otto when she saw him, and then she started crying. Because her papa was not there, Otto's papa took her in his arms and tried to shush her. "Let's get the hell out of here," Jumpers said, and Bartlett ordered them on.

That night, by moonlight and the feel of the ground against his spread fingers, Otto rubbed his magic dismembered finger and crept under the gaze of the sentries to Emma. He patted her face and made her smile. Then he felt his way across the ground to the girl with no nose. He took her by the hand, pulled his intact index finger to his lips to motion for her to be quiet. Then he motioned for her to follow him. They crept slowly through the moonlight, feeling the ground, to Thomas Jefferson. Together,

Otto and the no-nosed girl untied Thomas Jefferson. When Thomas Jefferson was free and staring at him, Otto pulled the no-nose girl's hand and placed it in Thomas Jefferson's. "Du Verstedst." Otto said to Thomas Jefferson, and Thomas Jefferson nodded his head. "You come get me later," Otto whispered. Again, Thomas Jefferson nodded. "Promise," Otto said.

"Shush," Thomas Jefferson said. Then Otto watched as Thomas Jefferson crawled into the dark with the no-nose girl following.

The next morning, Jumpers' rifle and horse were gone, and so were Thomas Jefferson and the girl with no nose. Jumpers demanded that they retrieve his property. Lieutenant Bartlett seemed happy that Thomas Jefferson was gone. So was Papa; he said to Otto, "It is good to be free of this slave business, but Otto what do you know of this?"

* * *

Back in Loyal Valley, Otto tried to learn his school lessons, but now, not only did he not trust the Deutsch and American words that the teacher used, but he distrusted what the words meant. All the other students were far ahead of him in their lessons. And none of the other students would talk to him, partially because he still wore his dismembered finger around his neck. Otto had scraped the rotted meat and gristle away, but the buckskin string that Thomas Jefferson had punched through the bone stayed intact. Otto then got another buckskin string and tied another of the bones of his fingers to the one attached. Only Emma Metzger liked Otto's necklace and talked to him, but she now had problems with school too, so Otto and Emma Metzger sat by themselves and tried to catch up.

After several months, Pappa said that Otto would stay home and do work and that Mama would teach him. But Mama looked at Otto in a strange way, and he could not concentrate, and he could not ask her why she looked at him so strangely. But he suspected that look had something to do with his mother watching his sister get hatcheted to death and Otto's coming back from the Nokonis. So Otto worked in the fields with Papa, tending the corn and cattle and his father's peach trees. But whenever he could, Otto would forget about work and run. First he would go fast, and then he would go far, always in the direction that the Comanches had carried him. When he got tired, he would walk back to his father's house to be scolded for risking another abduction by the savages.

And at night, Papa would read in Deutsch to Otto from what Papa said was Goethe. And then he would tell the stories that he had just read in English. That way Otto could learn the English. Soon Papa gave up teaching him at all. On his last attempt, Papa looked intently at Otto and asked him, "Otto is it that you are an idiot and have been this whole time?"

Otto answered, "I just don't like words, Papa. I like things."

"We were free-thinkers in Germany," Papa said. "And now you tell me you don't like words."

"I don't know which words or how to use them. There are too many," Otto said.

Papa did not scold him, but Papa told Otto that he would have to become a common laborer for hire once he got older. What Papa meant, what Otto could see was that, with first his brother and now Gertrude dead, Otto was responsible for his family's being good people and that Otto would fail to keep the family good people.

So on a spring day, when Otto was among the pink, blue, and yellow flowers, looking at the ground, more dark arms seized him. This time Otto almost welcomed the seizure. He let it take him. But the person behind the arms grunted and dropped Otto. "You gotten big," Thomas Jefferson said. Otto held up the bones that had been his finger.

"So them bones been protecting you?" Otto nodded. "You gotten any better with words?" Otto shook his head.

Thomas Jefferson looked anxiously around, then sat. "I come here to kill that Jumpers, but I figure ain't no use stirring up people against me." Otto touched his nose. "She living in a village with Black Seminoles down in Mexico," Thomas Jefferson said.

Otto thought to make the words. "So you take me?"

"So I take you," Thomas Jefferson said.

Otto climbed on behind Thomas Jefferson, and later in the day Thomas Jefferson stole a horse for Otto to ride and some food for them both. And they rode into the land that, years before, the Spanish named the Comanchería.

Playing Scared

It was during the 1981 oil show when I tried to fix Danny Fowler's killing. Ever two years, the high rollers from the oil patches across the country would hold an international oil show in Odessa, Texas. That meant lots of gambling, drinking, and whoring. During that week-long show, Odessans said there was more whores in Odessa per capita than any place in the world. You could pull off Second Street, and the whores would just run out in front of your car, press their cleavage against your windshield, and lick at your side mirror with long, tip-curled tongues. Flashing a badge would keep them off your car. Only telling them you had no money would get them to turn their mini-skirted, oversized asses to you and saunter off to another car.

That's how it operated. You drive up, do your whore shopping, and she takes you into one of the cheap motels. Of course the high-rollers running the oil show over at the fairgrounds had their tents, trailers, and hotels rooms. Their parties and their whores were invitation only. But if you weren't such a high roller, you had Second Street. The Odessa Police and the Ector County Sheriff's department wasn't about to stop the party despite what the Baptists and Church of Christers said.

This was the boomtime. People come from all over the country to work the oilfields. They pushed right out of the city limits into West Odessa, which was just barely paved streets, gravel parking lots, cinder block or trailer homes (sometimes tents or RVs), and mean bars. At nights, wound up, energized roughnecks with money in their pockets would drive around looking for whores, trouble, or just something to do. Sometimes, out of boredom or frustration, they'd just pull their guns out their pickups and start shooting up in the air. Besides whores, we had more murders per capita than anyplace else in the country. We even topped drug smuggling Miami. Like the other murders, Danny Fowler's killing had a lot to do with the whores and the oil boom.

Some mud tester on his way to the rig, driving on a dirt road off

Crane highway, found Danny's body just after sunrise. The mud tester was not yet in Crane County, so his 911 call got sent to the Ector County Sheriff's office. The Sheriff's Department sent a senior deputy, Bobby Cooksey—and me. The Crane County Sheriff, Travis Ashton, pulled up to our squad car. We all got out at once and hunched our shoulders to the wind and cold that was left from a norther the night before. We looked down into a new-dug pipeline ditch and saw the body. A tumbleweed blew into the ditch, hung for a while on Danny's face, tried to make it up the other side of the ditch, but then rolled back and settled back on Danny's face. We looked at each other, then back at the body. Bobby Cooksey dipped his foot into the ditch and scooted the tumbleweed off Danny's face with the pointed toe of one of his boots.

We did what we knew we was eventually going to have to do. We slid into the ditch and looked at the body. There wasn't no blood, no puncture wound, just lots of bruises on his face and chest. His shirt was ripped open. His camel hair sportcoat was wrapped around one arm. He was missing one of his Bass Wejuns shoes. "Looky here," Bobby Cooksey said, stood, and walked a little way toward the direction Danny's head was pointing. He bent over and picked up a key with a long red motel key fob attached to it. He held it up for us to see. We climbed back out of the ditch. "I'd think that ditch and the angle of his body puts him in Ector County," Travis Ashton said.

"He's ours," Bobby Cooksey said and poked the toe of his boot into the dirt. He stopped staring at the toe of his boot and pushed the brim of his black cowboy hat up farther on his head.

We heard a whine coming from the distance. "Ambulance," Bobby said. And Travis and I just mouthed the word *ambulance.* "He's beat to death," Bobby said. "We're looking for his red Mustang convertible," Bobby added.

"How you know he drives a convertible Mustang?" Travis asked.

"He's Mina Fowler's boy."

"Mina Fowler's boy?" Travis Ashton asked. Bobby nodded and sized me up. "Well, then I'm sure he's in Ector County," Travis Ashton said.

"And the Sheriff is called his Momma, and she ain't none too pleased, but she don't want to talk."

"I'd imagine not," Travis Ashton said. "Seeing her boy is dead and beat to death."

"Of course, it's that," Bobby said. "But it's dead like this bothers her," Bobby added. "She don't want much done."

"What do you mean?"

"She wants no news." When Ashton and I both looked up at him, Bobby explained some more. "She don't want nobody to know how he died."

"I'm sure it's an Ector County matter," Travis said. They both looked at me. And I shoveled some dirt with the toe of my boot and watched it, so I didn't have to look at them. "Justin, are you up to this?" Bobby asked.

"I seen bodies before," I said

"I mean investigating. Are you up to looking into this?"

I pulled my head up from my boot and looked at both older men. "Me?" was all I could say.

"His momma don't want headlines. Don't want to talk. But we need to look into it. Just kind of for perfunctory sake. You figure you could look into it?"

"I ain't got much of any experience," I said. "And don't we have some guys who do the investigating?"

"They're busy investigating. All I asked was could you look into it, not solve anything."

"Sure," I found myself saying. And we all watched as a tumbleweed loaded with paper and Styrofoam hopped past us in the wind.

My job was mainly arresting drunks, making them pour out the beer or booze in their cars, and then asking them to drive on home, and then telling them don't stop for another one. Sometimes, out in West Odessa, I'd stop a bar fight, clean up after one, or get in one while it was going on and I'm trying to arrest somebody. Then I would go home and tell my wife about police work. But here was a chance to really detect something. I wasn't ready.

My temperament, talent, and predisposition didn't suit me being a police officer. My talent, temperament, and predisposition didn't really suit much of anything. I had been a football player, not even at Permian High School and winning state championships every other season, but at Odessa High, the school across town, the one that lost. Then I tried college ball, but that didn't work out so good, so I became a deputy sheriff.

I slid back into the ditch, squatted by the body, and looked through the tumbleweed into Danny Fowler's open eyes. I guess I was trying to detect something. Danny Fowler must've hurt. He must've been all battered up inside. When I stood up, I felt like I had to help him even though he was dead. I felt like telling this to Travis Ashton and Bobby Cooksey, but they were walking back toward their cars.

I scampered out of the ditch and ran over the loose gravel and caliche to catch up with Bobby Cooksey. "Anything else you can tell me?"

Bobby reached into his pocket and pulled out the motel key and the fob. "Him or who beat him must of dropped it. If it was them, they couldn't find it in the dark." He handed it to me. "Probably one of them cheap places on Second Street running whores for the oil show."

I looked at him smiling. "Well, I'll start looking," I said.

"Don't get your hopes up. That motel and whores ain't the whole answer." He dug at dirt with his boot toe and said to the dirt, "Start with Mina Fowler. She might tell you what you need to know. Then you decide you want to keep looking." He turned from me, walked to his car, got in, and kicked up dirt and gravel while I stared after him with the key between my fingers and the fob dangling from them.

* * *

Bobby Cooksey had all but told me to forget the case. And I was full aware of my limitations. But I was thinking of advancement. I had a new wife, and we was talking about a family. We lived in a tiny and old house off Adams street. It was in a bad neighborhood. And before we could move out and start a family in a proper neighborhood, we needed money. My wife was a doctor's secretary and made more than me. She let me know that fact real often. She'd slump her shoulders or cock her head and lean on one hip to let me know without saying I had ought get a better job. What I didn't tell her was I had probably peter-principled myself right to the very top of what I could do. But if I could find Danny Fowler's killer, maybe I could prove to myself and my new wife that I could stretch my limitations a little farther and become a constructive part of the community with smart and handsome kids making good grades in good schools.

Mina Fowler lived just across the county line in a near sixty-year old two-story ranch house. She was Ector and Crane county nobility. Her grandfather had come to the area in a wagon, bought rangy cows, and made himself a herd. Then he bought more land, and that land had oil under it. And so Mina Fowler's daddy and then she became rich. Three worthless husbands had left her. She had a daughter's husband running the family business and making her richer. Now she had dead Danny.

My Ector County deputy sheriff's car kicked up a high wake of dust as I drove down the long dirt road to Mina Fowler's house. I had to steer around some of the mostly ornamental cows she kept around her house, probably for the sake of her father and grandfather.

I pulled up in front of the porch, knocked the heels of my boots against her wooden porch to shake the dust off, and rang the doorbell. A handsome older woman in jeans, boots, a shining red satin blouse and a glass of vodka in her hand answered the door. As soon as I got my business out of my mouth, she tried to shut the door. I put up my hand to hold the door open, and she let me follow her into her living room. "Sit," she commanded, and I did, on her red leather sofa. She sat in her recliner across from me and sipped at her vodka. "I told those other guys that I've got nothing to say. So what am I going to tell you?"

"I got to ask," I said.

She smiled. "I am not oil rich. I am cattle rich. But oil has made me wealthy. I stay here because the wealth gives me some power. My money makes people listen. So I don't want an investigation. I've told the Odessa Chief of Police and the Ector County Sheriff to leave the case exactly where it is: Danny's dead."

"But you know he was killed?"

"Of course I know he was killed." She sipped her vodka and waved her glass around, sloshing some of the vodka on her lap and the arm of her recliner. "Didn't they tell you anything?"

"I want to find the killer."

Mina laughed. "How was Danny dressed?"

"Nice shirt. Sportscoat. One of his shoes was gone."

"What you saw was his uniform. He'd put on an expensive camel hair coat and cruise. You know what I'm saying?"

"He'd drive around?"

"So to speak." Her brows knit together, and I could see that her eyes were red. "I may seem cavalier, but I spent the morning crying. Still I know what happened. I don't need to know the specifics."

"You want to tell me what happened?"

"The Odessa police have picked Danny up several times now, dressed just as he was, knocked out, drunk, bloodied or all three because he'd grabbed some cowboy or roughneck's crotch. Maybe somewhere, maybe once in awhile, maybe just often enough to give him hope, a cowboy or roughneck returned the favor. But mostly, they beat the shit out of him." She looked over her glass to ask if I was getting it.

I rubbed the top of one boot against my pant leg. "But don't you want the killer?"

"I want the killer dead, but I don't want people to know how Danny died. You starting to pick up what I'm saying?"

"There was a murder."

"And people in law enforcement are friends of mine and cases are unsolved. Now you go tell Bobby Cooksey you had no better luck than him."

I did as I was told. And Bobby Cooksey chuckled and said he was too old and too long in the area to piss off Mina Fowler, but if I was young and dared stick my cock out, then I should go for it. "It just pains a cop to let a crime sit, but watch your cock," Cooksey said to me as if to explain what I should do.

So I went home. And I found my new wife already in her bathrobe, sipping a beer and watching some movie on HBO. I couldn't tell what she watched. I just heard stuff blowing up. She rolled her head toward me. I said, "You think we could do without the HBO? It's another twenty bucks a month."

She rolled her head back toward the TV. "I'm worn out. Overtime again. I don't even know what I'm watching. But I like these movies better than regular TV."

I stepped across our living room in three steps and sat beside her, "Want me to go get some dinner?"

"I'll eat some peanut butter and white bread," she said.

"I want something more," I said.

"There's some can spaghetti or something," she said.

I stood up, stepped to the kitchen for my own beer, and looked back over my shoulder at her. I still thought she was beautiful.

That night, I groped her a little. She reached back and rubbed down there. But that's as far as we got.

* * *

The next day, instead of eating Frosty Flakes, I ate a real breakfast that cost real money at a Pancake House on Second Street. As I shoveled the yellow yokes of eggs mixed with syrup soaked pancakes into my mouth, I watched the wind blow the trash down Second Street. This town was where I grew up. As the trash gained speed, it probably blew past my mother looking out her kitchen window and drinking her coffee and eating her oatmeal. I didn't know where my father was. My older brother foolishly tried to hold up a convenience store with his worthless friends right after they quit high school. So he had done some prison time and was floating around the country trying to find what construction work he could before his body gave out. So my pedigree didn't allow me no better life than what I had. With my pedigree, I was probably lucky to be where I was.

As I was scooping up the last of my meal, a short man with a big old belly and a frayed and faded Odessa High letter jacket eyed me, then came up to me. "Justin Brady?" he asked. I nodded. "Whatever become of you?"

I recognized him. I had played high school football with him at Odessa High School. We was the Bronchos. We never knew our mascot was misspelled. "You were a star."

I shrugged. "I went to Sul Ross and tried to play, but I was slow and too small, so now I'm a deputy sheriff." There it was. I had covered my life.

"I thought you was going to be somebody famous."

"You never know," I said.

"Well, you know, I just never got that college scholarship, so I stuck around. A welder now." We both shrugged. He left. I couldn't remember his name. I tried. But all I could remember were the sticker burrs. In my backyard and on the practice fields, the stickers burrs and goatheads took over in the summer when the sun killed the grass. So from the time I was six to eighteen, my hands, fingers, knees, and elbows were filled with the festering sores from sticker burr splinters. I held my hands up. What I had to account for progress in my life was soft hands unlike my brother, my mother, my classmates, and probably my father. When I got my breakfast ate, I went out looking for the right motel. I guessed right.

The First Quality Motel had a sign on Second Street, but it sat behind Second Street, on Third Street: the perfect place to run whores. The kid in the office stumbled over his words when I held up the key in front of him and asked about the murder. We both knew he wasn't going to be able to talk, so he led me down the row of 1950s style rooms. As we passed by one, I yelled to him to stop. I stepped up to the open door. Inside, several guys was washing a wall with soapy water and rolling up a carpet they had just pried loose from the floor.

I turned back to the kid, and he led me to the end of the row. We stood in front of large duplex. He knocked at the door. We both heard a voice yell, "It's open." He opened the door for me, and I stepped in.

In front of me was a desk, but I didn't look at it. I looked around the apartment. It had red shag carpet. It had a gold chandelier light. It had gold lamps shaped like naked women holding up red lamp shades. The walls was some sort of textured gray or brown. In back of the desk was a rock wall. Behind it, I figured was a kitchen. To a side was a dining room with a gold arch over it. I sat down in front of the desk. "This is my home. I live here," a woman's voice came from behind the desk.

There was smoke in my face, and I looked through it to see a figure pulling a cigarette away from her face. When the smoke cleared, I saw that it was indeed a woman. She had earrings and lipstick, but her hair was sheared into an old-style crew cut—punk style. She also had a scar slanting across her forehead and down her left cheek. "Now can I help you?" she asked.

"My name is Deputy Justin Brady. I'm with the Ector County Sheriff's Department, and I want to ask a few questions about what I am supposing took place in that room you're washing out."

The woman raised her cigarette to her mouth, sucked in on it, then exhaled. "You ever try to get blood out of a carpet? It ain't easy."

"So what happened in there?"

"You come in here all cocky instead of polite like you're supposed to do, so you tell me. All I know is I got blood on a carpet."

I held up the motel key. "We found this on a dead man. His name was Danny Fowler. He comes from prominent people." The woman took another puff. "I don't smoke," I said and coughed. The woman ground the cigarette out in an ashtray.

"My name is Dee Price. I sort of manage this place. I've been in this town several years. I've heard of Danny Fowler. That's all I know."

"Ma'am, you know, you really ought to help us."

"Why?"

"'Cause we're the police."

"That's why I don't want to help you."

I felt flummoxed. I didn't know what more to say, so I looked at the red and gold room. I didn't want to just leave. "Look, at me," the woman said. She half-way smiled at me. "Look at this." She pointed to the scar on her face. She undid the button to her blouse and held the right side open. "Look," she said. "Don't look away." She wore no bra. Where there should've been a tit, there was just some ugly read scars. "I'm just thirty-six years old, but I've got these two scars. The first one an ex-husband gave me when he tried to break a whiskey bottle over my head. They don't break. That's just on TV. And just this last year, at the county's expense, I had a mastectomy. I keep my hair short now. It kind of fits my altered gender image."

"I'm sorry for you illness. Your hairdo looks nice."

"That ain't why I'm showing you."

"Should you be smoking?" I asked.

"No, of course not," Dee Price said. "I'm just telling you that I can take trouble, but I don't want it. Second, I'm telling you that I will fight back. So why don't you look somewhere else?"

"'Cause we both know he was here."

"Is this investigation of yours going to be just a murder case?"

"What do you mean? That's what it is."

Dee dropped her eyes, like she was disappointed in me. "It's not going to turn into a vice case is it?"

"We don't have a vice squad at Ector County Sheriff's Department."

"You make me want a cigarette," Dee said and rubbed her palm over her short hair. "Are some Odessa cops going to come in here looking for crimes other than murder?"

"I work for the county."

"Justin, it's the oil show. I run whores. It's ironic, ain't it. I sell femininity. And whores have illegal habits. After the oil show is over, I'm going to be real quiet. In the meantime, you going to leave this an investigation and not a bust me?"

I stumbled as I tried to talk. "Yes," I said without knowing that I could keep the promise, but I knew the Sheriff's Department and the Odessa Police Department were already looking the other way.

She leaned back to look at me like she didn't trust me. She reached for a cigarette, tried to light it, but didn't. "Last time, I saw that key, Buffy St. Cloud had it. Don't make me regret this." She was almost pleading.

"Buffy St. Cloud?" I asked.

Dee frowned. "Justin, whores, like strippers, have fake names. Come back at five. Buffy'll be back by."

I drove back to the courthouse and called my wife. Michelle told me not to mind the investigation. She said he was dead. That was all. Think about my future, she said.

When I played football, I was an old style monster man. That's sort of like a strong safety. My job was to crouch in the backfield and wait for the run. And when I saw it coming, I was to run into the blocking and make the tackle. Most of the people running at me were bigger and stronger, but I had a talent of throwing myself into them. But as the running play was starting, as I saw the guards pulling, even as I was getting excited, I got scared, and I had to make myself run into what was stronger and faster. When the play was over, if nothing on me was broke, then I'd get excited.

Playing scared like that got me a chance at college, at Sul Ross State University, where I didn't have my fingers festering from sticker burrs. My freshman year at Sul Ross State University I had a small scholarship. My sophomore year, I had a bigger one. On the last game of my sophomore year, in the middle of the third quarter with Hardin-Simmons University beating us by twenty-one points, I saw the guards and running backs chugging around the end. I should've stayed where I was, given them the yards that no longer made no difference. Everybody else on my team was just standing still, but I run up into those that were bigger and faster and stronger, and I just buckled. It was a time before orthroscopic surgery, so I was finished with my sophomore year by the time my knee healed. But it did not heal good enough to play no more football. I'd played through my scaredness, thinking it would get me a degree and a better place in the world. But now, without that degree, I was even more scared.

So I went back to Odessa, worked in the oilfield a little, until a friend said he knew the sheriff and knew there were some deputy sheriff jobs. So I went back to school, the police academy at Odessa College, then got to be a deputy sheriff, but I was playing scared there too. And then I met Michelle. She was not the best looking, wanted only to get a little ahead in Odessa, no ambitions to go into the outside world, so I married. And again, I felt like I was waiting in the backfield for those that were handsomer, smoother, stronger, faster, better, smarter, quicker, or meaner than me.

* * *

At five-thirty, I was in Dee's office watching her as she paced, sucked in on a cigarette, and rubbed her crew-cut head. "You know this is likely to come to naught," she said.

"I want to find the killer."

When we heard a knock at the door, Dee said. "She came here from Lafayette, Louisiana looking for fast and easy money. She found fast and easy, but not enough money." She opened the door.

Buffy St. Cloud had on a mini-skirt that barely covered her butt. But then it was hardly a butt at all. Same with her chest. Just two mosquito bites, as they say. She had dirty blonde hair hanging in a couple of strings over her face. She was mostly a little girl trying real hard to play older and sexier. She swivelled her head between Dee and me. And Dee looked at me as she said, "You're not in trouble."

"A night or so ago, you had a guy, maybe. He had on Bass Weejuns, a sportcoat, a white shirt," I said.

"A fancy dresser," she said while looking up at Dee. "I seen him." She turned to me. "You ain't gonna turn me in or tell my momma?" she asked.

Dee sucked in on the cigarette. "You tell the man what you know."

Buffy hung her head and lowered herself into a chair across from the desk. I pulled another one up to her. She raised her head to look at me. "I'm really a good girl, so don't you go making judgments against me."

I might've well been talking to a child. She went on. "It was god-awful cold last night, first real norther of the season. And I thought about just staying by myself under a blanket. But I wandered out to the street. And this fast-looking car . . . "

"What kind of car?" I stopped her.

"A Camaro," she said, "or one of those Firebirds. No, a Camaro," She said.

"Could it have been a Ford Mustang?"

"Yeah, it could have been."

I scribbled that down. "Did you get a license plate?" Both Dee and Buffy looked at me like I was stupid.

"A fella like you described was driving. A stocky boy was sitting in the back. A boy with a cowboy hat was up in the passenger side. The fancy dresser paid."

I wanted to ask her how much, but I didn't. Instead, I gave a rough look to Dee. She turned her back to me and said, "Get on with your questioning, sheriff."

"You the sheriff?" Buffy asked.

"A deputy," I said.

"I take the boys to number three." She stopped, ducked her head.

"What happened?"

"What do you think happened?" Dee asked from behind me.

"They was in a partying mood. They all drank. Then, then we got to it. One, then the other."

"There were three."

"The sharp-dressed fella, he wasn't interested."

"He paid?"

Dee asked, "Did they seem like they all knew one another?"

"I'm asking the questions."

"Well, ask some good ones."

"The two boys knew each other. They talked about going to the Tank and eating steaks and drinking good liquor. Seems like they must've met the dresser there."

"Anything else they talked about?" I asked

"Work."

"Where was work?"

"They said something about a casing crew."

"How did they act around that fancy dresser?"

"Friendly like. And he was real friendly to them."

"How's that?"

"He'd whisper stuff to them. He'd pat their backs."

"Did they do anything to him?"

"I don't know. After a couple of hours I left," she dropped her head for the last time. "It was cold, and the wind was blowing trash and tumbleweeds down the street, but there was money to be made."

Buffy talked about her night, about her plans, about her money. She went on to beg me not to bust her, not to tell her momma, not to chase any of the boys away. "I'm a good girl. I really am. I mean to make some money for college."

"Are you even out of high school?"

She smiled and got up to leave without answering my question. When the door shut behind her, Dee Price said, "Whores! All of them got a sob story."

I looked at the gold arches, the red shag carpet, and the naked lady lamps and felt like I was going to start choking. "You need anymore help with your case?" Dee asked.

"I don't need any goddamn help," I said. "I got control of this."

"You don't look it." She sat behind her desk. "Those boys are just like her. This is a boomtown. It attracts young folks looking for quick money. If they killed him, they're gone. And you'll never find them."

"I'm going to the Tank."

"Wait," Dee said. "I know people." She called the Tank and talked to a waiter she knew.

The Tank was an old holding tank with a couple of windows cut into it, a round bar in its center, and tables surrounding that bar. And above the first floor is a second floor with the center cut out, so a customer can look down at the first floor. You could get a good steak and good liquor and drop a lot of oil field money at the Tank. Dee hung up the phone, folded her arms, and leaned across her desk. The scar across her face was a little lighter that the rest of her face. "My friend says he knew what Danny was up to. Or wishing. Or trying. He said he thought of warning the two boys. But they were noisy and acting bad, so he thought when they got what was coming, it'd be funny and serve them right."

"I'm still driving over there," I said.

"Want me to find out what casing grew they worked for?"

"I don't want you to do nothing."

"But you got to admit I helped." Dee eyed me. "You remember your promises and keep the law off of me." She folded her arms and glared at me. But then her face and her shoulders just sagged. She rubbed her head. The scar on her face made her look weak. "Please," she said.

I went to the Tank, but nobody remembered anything. Waiters, waitresses, and bartenders didn't see nothing or forgot. But one waiter let a comment slip out his mouth. "He got what he deserved if you ask me."

"You know Dee Price?" I asked him. He shrugged. "Could you give me a description of Danny Fowler?"

"Sure," he said.

"Could you describe the two boys he left with?" I asked.

"One had on a hat," he said. And that was all he said.

* * *

A month later, parts of Danny's red Mustang Convertible showed up in El Paso. My looking went on through the winter. Going to casing crew offices, asking who had left, begging for names, addresses, phone numbers of men who quit during the oil show, men who just hadn't showed for work. Driving by the addresses I did get. Talking to wives. Talking to pissed off men. Talking to more casing crews, mostly boys my age. Standing in the cold, three A.M. in the morning talking, sipping the cold coffee that my hand didn't shake out of the Styrofoam cup, while those boys poured cement down a hole. Nobody knew nothing. Meanwhile, Michelle is at home, and she stops talking to me.

I knew the answer. Men working on a casing crew are a step above roughnecks. A man can support a family real well with casing crew work, even if he won't see that family. A young, single man could finance himself for three our four years with a year or two of casing work. So the young men that killed Danny Fowler probably run as soon as they dumped his body. When the winds of spring blew the trash and tumbleweeds against the barbed wire fences, Bobby Cooksey ordered me to just give up on it. So I failed my one big chance and went back to being a cop and not a detective.

Like I did when I played football, when I tried to find Danny Fowler's killers, I was scared, but I threw myself into the bruising. I did him no good. I did me no good. I had stirred up shit. I had forced the Odessa City Police Department's hand. They had to investigate. But the city cops didn't do no better than me. They got embarrassed, so they busted Buffy St. Cloud.

So in my imagination, I replayed the crime. In my mind, Danny Fowler is in the condominium his mother bought for him, and he eyes himself in his full length mirror; he admires his Bass Wejuns, his pressed wool slacks, and his camelhair sportcoat. His hair goes over the tops of his ears and his forehead in waves. He is a good looking man, knows he is, admires himself. He is ready to go out.

It is a windy day with cold blowing in, but Danny drives his convertible red Mustang around town with the top down and turns up the collar of his camel hair sportcoat and wraps a wool throat-warmer scarf around his neck. He checks out Busby's, a small bar downtown. He drives by Graham Central Station, the large country-western disco out Grandview. He drives out to West Odessa, out to my jurisdiction, and looks at several small, mom-and-pop bars. Nothing there will do for the way he is dressed and what he wants. So he goes to the Tank.

At the Tank, he leans his back against the bar—a cigarette dangling out from his knuckles, one foot cocked behind his other leg, a wave of hair falling down on his forehead and looks for something. It ain't exactly sex he is looking for. It is something else too. It is some amusement, some story, something colorful, something relieving him of having to be him stuck in Odessa, Texas. A waiter who knows him comes up to him and says, "These are dangerous waters for you to be trolling in." Danny nods to agree with the bartender, and he sees these two boys sitting at a table, finishing off their steak and drinking single malt scotch to celebrate their luck in the oilfield. It is payday for them. They are starting to get loud. He walks toward their table, reaches in his pocket, pulls out two business cards saying he is in real estate, introduces himself to the boys, gives them his cards, says, "But real estate is not my real line of business."

The two boys do not tell him to fuck off and mind his own business as they would of if they was older and had been around as much as they thought. Instead, they listen. And Danny says, "For my real business, my main business, I manage strippers and whores."

The two boys have seen the laughing groups of men surrounded by girls in slinky black, green, and red dresses hugging the forms of their bodies, and they see those girls squeezing those exaggerated bodies into the laps of those laughing men. And they figure that those girls got to those men somehow. They figure Danny is how.

And Danny smiling, dressing like he was from college, acting all smooth-like, his cigarette dangling from his lip, his movie-star looks, his business cards, all guarantee them two boys that he is their man.

Danny buys them some more scotch. Then he recommends one of his favorite scotches. Soon the boys are banging the table with the flats of their hands yelling for pussy.

I'll call the two boys Randy and Mel. They are younger than me, maybe two or three years out of high school. Unlike me, when they get out of high school there is an oil boom, and the legal age for drinking is eighteen. So they become roughnecks. They work hard, party harder, get on a casing crew, have money to burn if they want. They yearn bad for the pussy that they yell for. And so they want to believe Danny.

Mel is short, squat, made to look like he's a body-builder by the hard work he has done. He is the skeptical one or he is just scared. He just ain't grown up that much yet, still a little shy around the company he keeps and places he goes. He says nothing about Danny's offer, just eyes the business cards and Danny's sharp figure. The hard work has made Randy lean like a cowboy. He likes the way he looks, so he has bought him a new silver belly cowboy hat. It sits proper, crown down, brim up, on the seat of the chair next to him. "So where's these whores and strippers?" he asks after more scotch.

Mel mumbles, shut up, "This guy ain't no pimp."

"You're right," Danny says. "I'm a friend. I know the bartender. Let's get some beers and paper bags and go find some of my ladies."

Randy gives a whoop. Mel just watches. They get into Danny's red convertible Mustang. Mel scrunches himself up and sits in back. Randy gets in the front passenger side. Mel is silent. Danny has the top down now. Randy whoops more as they drive to Second Street and splashes his beer in Danny's red convertible Mustang.

Danny finds Buffy St. Cloud trying to stand still in the blowing cold, hugging herself, trying to keep her short skirt pulled over her freezing ass. She looks like some Greek goddess to Randy and Mel. They go to room number three at the First Quality Motel. They all step in and rub the wind out of their hair and clothes as people are prone to do in West Texas. They drink some more. They eye each other. Only Randy and Buffy's eyes stick, don't roam. So Randy has his turn with Buffy. And Mel and Danny watch.

Then Mel, a little scared, a lot drunk, has his turn with Buffy. "You could act like it was a pleasure," Buffy says when Mel rolls off her. When Danny pays her and refuses his turn, they start poking him with their elbows and laugh at him. Danny blames it on the liquor. Danny has more scotch, more beer, and Buffy, feeling some relief from being stuck in Odessa, drinks with them.

But nobody can stop being them, so Buffy stumbles out after several drinks, thinking she can find some more customers, but she finds she has to puke. Inside the room, Danny sits beside Randy, tells him that they don't really need any more women. Randy wonders for a moment what Danny is talking about, "Well, hell yes we do. Let's get us another one. I still got lead in my pencil." It is Mel who figures out what Danny is asking. And Danny, to let them know for sure, slides his palm inside Randy's thigh and then up.

That same high school urge that made me want to try playing football, made be head into the oncoming line of blockers, and even made me kind of enjoy the knocking heads, even if I was scared, makes Randy hit Danny on the corner of his head. Mel says, "Goddamn, Queer," and hits Danny too.

Danny holds on to his head, smiles, says, "Boys? A boy has to try. Why do you blame me?" He looks at them like he is begging them.

One or the other, by himself, Mel or Randy would've quit hitting Danny and left. But together they whale him. They scream, "Fucking A. Fucker." They are excited, like they are winning a football game. They high-five each other when they feel they've tired themselves out. Then they notice that Danny isn't moving. There's a small puddle of blood on the carpet.

Though they are drunk, they keep drinking. They try to think. They pull Danny out to his car and lose a shoe on the way. They both get in the Mustang. They dump Danny's body off just outside the city limits. This a boom time, so they know a guy who moves stolen cars. Randy delivers it. Mel picks him up. By the time I am looking at Danny's body, they are driving east and west outside of town, each one swearing that he's never going think about Odessa for the rest of his life.

In my imagination, I make me smarter. So I find an address, go to an apartment, ask around, get a name, find a registration for a car, check some chop shops in town, find the guy that chopped Danny's car, get a description of Mel, call towns along I-20 East and West from El Paso to Forth Worth. I find Mel's parents in Jal, New Mexico. They give me a phone number. I trace it to a Dallas. I arrest Mel, and he informs on Randy. They get convicted of voluntary manslaughter.

* * *

Danny's murder was my last real case. West Texas is a good area for cops. Most cases are simple. You get a call from a woman screaming about her no good, two-timing, son-of-a-bitch husband. You drive to the crumbling house or trailer out in West Odessa, outside of city limits. There you find the husband dead and bleeding on the living room carpet and the woman holding a smoking gun, probably a birthday present he bought for her. That's the kind of crimes I solved from then on.

The oil boom busted, and Odessa bars put signs on their windows that said: "An Oil field Prayer: Please God, give us another oil boom, and I promise not to piss this one away." Without oil money hiding the demand for whores, the city finally busted Dee for good. I went by her motel to say goodbye. She said she was in good health. She still smoked.

My marriage busted too. Michelle asked me what I was thinking, urged me to get a job, not a hobby, asked me what I wanted of myself. We kind of forgot why we picked each other to marry. We just didn't know what we were doing. As we got smarter, we divorced.

I married again, had children, and got them mostly grown. I didn't quit my job, but this time I worked harder and was more careful, played scared, but didn't run into the line. I arrested drunks, investigated simple murders. But the movie in my mind replays a lot. I'll bet Danny's murderers, Randy and Mel, whoever they are, play more real movies in their minds about what they done to Danny. They've probably got grown children too, and I bet those two men can't stop thinking they gave their grown kids that thing that made them murder Danny Fowler. All I am, all I gave my kids, is scared.

Danny Fowler surely knew that he was in West Texas and knew what a dangerous game he was playing. But as surely as he knew West Texas, he just couldn't stop being himself. Randy and Mel, whoever his murderers were, should've known that nobody was just going to treat them to what their hormones were demanding, still, those hormones demanded. They shouldn't of hit him, or should've stopped hitting him. Still, back then, that's what you did to a queer. I shouldn't of played football. Shouldn't of married Michelle. Should've listened to Bobby Cooksey and never investigated Danny Fowler's murder.

From when I am telling this, the boom is come back. It is tamer this time, and we're not all pissing our money away. But some things don't change. My children and Danny's murderer's children will make mistakes like ours. Those mistakes are taking place all over town. They say you can't prosecute stupidity. But as time goes on, I wish you could.

Dee Price's Story

Sometimes, to impress those of us who knew her, besides the obvious scar across her forehead, made by a whiskey bottle, Dee would show us the hidden scar left by her mastectomy. To those of use who knew her, Dee Price always said that the curious thing about johns, no matter how rich or poor, cleaned up or trashy, was that most kept their socks on. Maybe they wanted to be able to grab their shoes or boots, slip them on, and run out the window or the backdoor in case a cop or a wife was coming. Their pants didn't seem to matter as much. Then, she'd tell us that if you looked close into a whore's eyes, you could see if she had lost her soul or not. Most, she said, had.

Dee could comment from experience. She first got that experience in San Antonio when she was young and teeth-itching good looking. By the time she got to Odessa, Texas she was running whores, as Texans say, but not whoring herself. After several years in Odessa, she diversified from whoring and got fairly wealthy. She bought low-down, failing buildings with bad plumbing, mostly out in West Odessa, and rented them out as bars, nasty video shops, or mom and pop restaurants. But she retained the vending machines and the rights to their profits. So that way, while her renters' businesses were failing, she was making money. Whether running whores or buildings and vending machines, Dee Price was good at coping with the rotating labor pool while making money. In our world, Dee Price was a success. But because the statute of limitations doesn't run out for an assassination, not many Odessans knew how Dee Price came into her batch of big money in the Odessa drinking and whoring world. The city police and the sheriff's department certainly didn't know, although some cops and deputies surely had their suspicions.

Dee Price was never only a whore. In the mid-sixties, young and pretty, with a body that curved in the right ways to meet the fashions of the time, always adapting, Dee Price started out as an exotic dancer in San Antonio. It was still the dark edges in Texas, the time before 1973, when

45

liquor by the drink was legalized. Until then, liquor drinkers brought a bottle in a brown paper bag into a bar, sat it on the table, and ordered set-ups: cokes and ice. Of course, a few places claimed to be private clubs and charged a dollar membership so they could sell you an overpriced bottle themselves.

Dee eventually worked her way to a job as a go-go dancer in a bamboo cage at Bwana Dik's on the San Antonio River Walk. Bwana Dik's was just a bit sleazy but was also new and hip and swinging in the sixties. Both men and women drank while girls in bikinis shook their assess in cages. Some cages lowered right down from the ceiling. Bwana Dik's was downtown and catered to the high rollers who came off the street. On the backside it faced the river. By the mid-sixties in preparation for San Antonio's "Hemisfair," the fashionable and safe parts of the River Walk had spread beyond Casa Rio and under Bwana Dik's balcony. On hot summer nights Dee liked to go out onto the small balcony in her bikini, have a smoke, and cool off in the night air. She knew that airmen on leave from Lackland Air Force Base and teenage boys gathered on this edge of the nice and slightly dangerous part of the river and gazed up at Bwana Dik's balcony aching for the prizes in Bwana Dik's cages. When she stood out on the balcony on these hot San Antonio summer nights, Dee, one of Bwana's Dik's best dancers—not because of her dancing or even her body but because of the way she looked at the customers—would squirm or flex and look directly at those Air Force or high school kids and make promises with her eyes, her smile, and her body. She was always advertising. So sometimes the airmen or high schoolers would pull out their fake I.D.s, or the doorman would look the other way, and they came into Bwana Dik's and spent all of what little money they had watching Dee and the other dancers.

Bwana Dik's had an ex-semi-pro football player, six foot six, Charlie Brodsky as a bouncer. Charlie could take somebody down or out, with a tackle, a fist, a knife, or a gun. Charlie had been to prison once, looked it, and wasn't afraid to go back. If a patron really needed a girl, really wanted to see all of what he saw dancing in the bamboo cage, then he could screw his courage into himself and ask Charlie. If Charlie saw no danger for the girl, he would collect an appropriate amount from the gentleman, take out a cut for himself, save the rest for the girl, and then introduce the gentleman to the girl in the cage. Charlie would then call a special number at the Lee or Bluebonnet Hotels, inexpensive hotels but not yet gone to seed. The girl would sit with the gentleman, or gentlemen, during her break, and then after she got off work, the gentleman or gentlemen would escort her to a reserved room at the Bluebonnet or Lee Hotels. If a girl had any problems, the gentleman or gentlemen answered to Charlie. Dee was one of the most popular dates.

On a summer evening with no date after work, after showing off the curves of her body to the high school boys and the airmen, Dee was sitting by the bar rubbing her bare feet after wearing high heels with all her dances. She was already a veteran at Bwana Dik's, was smart, and knew the way Bwana Dik's and the rest of world at that time worked. Charlie Brodsky came to Dee and asked her if she really trusted him. Dee said she did. Charlie studied her. "Just how tough are you?" he asked her. "You act tough."

"You checking me out or what?" Dee asked.

"Pinky Adams wants to talk to you," Charlie said.

Pinky Adams was really Loren Adams, but he lost that name when he got a lot of money. Pinky had controlling interest in Bwana Dik's and a lot of other places. So Charlie escorted Dee up the stairs of Bwana Dik's to the third floor office. He knocked; another big guy let them in. This was Pinky's gambling room: high rollers, hot shots, people who couldn't afford to lose but did anyway. Charlie sometimes collected. And Charlie and Dee made their way across the gambling floor with its poker games, roulette wheels, and craps table—all illegal in Texas, along with the liquor by the drink Pinky served—to a door on the opposite wall. Charlie knocked, a voice sounded, and Charlie escorted Dee into the next part of her life.

With a drinker's explosion of veins in his nose and cheeks, Pinky looked pink. He had on a powder blue polyester suit, white shirt, and pink tie. He had on white shoes and matching white belt. He escorted Charlie and Dee to his desk and then walked around it to sit behind it. They all stared at each other, and then Pinky got down to business. "Dee, Charlie here tells me you're a bright girl. So I want you to answer me straight up."

"I don't plan to do anything but," Dee said.

Pinky's face dropped into a frown, then he managed to push his mouth into a smile while his eyes still frowned. "What plans you got?"

"What do you mean?"

"I mean, you not thirty yet, but you close, right? So what you going to do at the end of your dancing days? What you going to do if the men don't want to pay top dollar for the pleasure of your favors?"

"Try something else, I guess," Dee said. Charlie looked at her like he was trying to tell her to watch her mouth.

"Well, I can help with that something else," Pinky said. "Now you listen for a while before you talk. Then you think real hard for a minute or two and then you talk. Now, what I'm offering you, what I'm about to say, I never said. But I got a business associate down in Monterrey in Nuevo León, Mexico. He's sending a negotiator of sorts to see me. I want to entertain the negotiator, but I don't want to see him."

Dee, of course, a smart girl, could guess where this was going, but she was still young, had a few options in her life, and so she screwed her butt into the seat of her chair and lightly bit the side of her tongue. Pinky continued, "I asked Charlie to take care of this negotiator in order to send a message to my associate in Mexico. He's got a plan, but it involves you." Pinky cleared his throat and looked down. He was the one tongue-tied, but Dee dared not speak yet.

"She's tough enough," Charlie said. "Just is she willing?"

Dee didn't know who to answer to: Charlie or Pinky. "Can you kill a man?" Pinky asked.

Dee started to answer, but Pinky was too quick for her to get any words out of her mouth, "Now you think, then think some more before you say something. What's at the end of this deal is a good job working for me or a big ol' lump of money for you to use as wish. Hell, go to college and become a cheerleader, stay drunk for a year or two. But you take the money, I don't know you. You're gone. Now have you thought?" Pinky said.

He held up his index finger. On it, Dee noticed, was an over-sized diamond ring. "One, you going to do this or no?"

Dee knew enough of the world she was in to know that she could not say, "no." She already knew too much. So Dee said, "Yes."

"You going to take the job or the money?"

Dee figured she had a choice here, and she knew if there was any room to wiggle in Pinky's offer, this was the place. "The money. But, I'd like to see some up front," Dee said.

Charlie turned his head away from Dee. Pinky looked at her with his forced smile. "Okay then. This is all I want to see of you. You and Charlie plan this out and get it done. Charlie'll bring you some money in a day or two, and when I read about things in the paper or better yet hear about them, then you'll get the rest of the money."

Dee fidgeted before she left. When Charlie motioned for her to go, she stood, but she asked, "What kind of job would it have been?"

Pinky looked bored now. "A suitable one."

Dee nodded said, "I thought so," under her breath, then followed Charlie back through the gambling.

* * *

Charlie told Dee, "A gun has problems. Even with a silencer, someone might hear something. It's bulky. Then you might drop a casing somewhere. Someone finds it. A knife is bloody and messy, but easier to hide, and you don't leave as much evidence." Dee didn't dare disagree because she had nothing to say, because she knew she was in way over her head. So Charlie peeled the rind off of cantaloupe and had Dee slicing into it with a sharp switchblade. He coached her, told her to apply just the right amount of pressure, got her to pull the blade toward herself, to slice, not cut—well, just like a cantaloupe.

Charlie fixed what could be problems. When Dee brought a client to the Lee Hotel, she always gave the night manager at the desk a knowing smile. And he would courteously smile back and take the client's money. But Charlie sweetened the night manager's smile with an envelope filled with a bunch of bills. He told the manager the money was for forgetting things if the police or anyone asked about what might happen. And he told the manager that he would call soon and ask for a particular room on the third floor and that the manager would have that room available no matter what.

He did the same for the maid who cleaned up the third floor. Her money was for to show up early, clean the room, and not talk. He "bought" the mattress from the maid and wrapped a plastic sheet around it and stuffed a switchblade underneath the mattress.

Charlie took Dee out for a meal at Casa Rio. They sat by the river. Charlie smoked and flicked his cigarette ashes into the river. He looked at Dee almost tender-like and reached to put his fingertips on top of her hand. Instead of jerking her hand away from him, Dee held her hand still while Charlie stroked the top of it. "Now you can do this?" he asked.

"We've been practicing."

"But I never asked you, could you do it?"

"A little late now," Dee said. She tried to smile. Charlie wouldn't even look at her.

"I'll be at the door listening, my gun ready. And I'm going to have some help with me." Dee nodded and grew more worried.

"I almost wished you'da said no when Pinky asked," Charlie said. He pulled his head up to look at Dee. "I don't like to think it of you."

Dee said nothing, but she took her opposite hand and patted Charlie's hand, the one that was feeling the back of her hand. They sat like that for awhile, Dee realizing that big tough Charlie might have felt something for her. "Once I got into Pinky's office, did I ever really have a choice?"

"I guess not," Charlie said. "But I could have covered for you." Dee got a little fond of Charlie, but she also realized that, if she wanted, she could have gotten him to do most anything for her. Of course, maybe he was getting her to do what Pinky wanted.

The associate from Mexico's representative was big man named Saucedo. He wore white dress pants and a short-sleeved, lime-green mock turtleneck pullover with elastic at the bottom. He sat with Charlie while Dee danced on a table. After her dances, Dee sat at their table. Dee felt Saucedo's breath on the side of her face as she leaned over to hug him. And she looked at Charlie's wide eyes when he watched her hug Saucedo. As the night went on, Dee watched Saucedo's eyes grow blurry from the booze that Charlie poured down him. After her last set, she sat with them and coaxed Saucedo to drink even more. The plan went perfect. Dee's service was compliments of Pinky. And together Saucedo and Dee walked arm in arm with Dee faking sexiness while Charlie trailed behind in the late night downtown shadows and alleys. When they got to the lobby of the Lee Hotel, the night clerk gave Dee a knowing smile.

Once in the third floor room, Dee stepped into the light coming in from the downtown lights. And she took off all of her clothes. Saucedo did the same, except for his socks. In the faint light, Dee saw that his thick whisker went all the way down. The hair on his shoulders was as curly as but not as thick as the hair on his chest. She stepped in that runway-model, playboy-bunny fashion toward him and hugged him. He was sweaty too. And his breath smelled like the combination of liquors he had drunk.

She pulled him on to the bed and on top of her. He entered her in all kinds of ways. She was tempted to just let her mind go somewhere else, but she needed her concentration for what she agreed to do. So she felt every part of him on or in her body. And a chill went through her because she was thinking about what she was about to do. And he said, "Wow, that a way, baby."

She pushed and shoved, but he grunted and was not about to give way. So she said, "Let me get on top." He didn't quite understand, so she pushed and poked and shoved until she was straddling him. She bent to him, kissed him just under his ear, reached in between the plastic-lined mattress and the bedsprings, felt the switch blade, and pulled it out.

She pulled herself up away from his face. He was smiling, motioning with just his eyes to do some more. She flicked the blade out, raised the knife, and pushed it through the suddenly thick air toward his throat. But she didn't press in and then pull like she'd done with the cantaloupe, she swiped. And with one great jerk, Saucedo flipped her off him. He got to his feet, holding his throat, gurgling, blood seeping through his fingers.

He inched toward her like one of those horror movie monsters —Frankenstein or the Mummy—stiff-legged, one arm in front of him. But when his feet caught in his pants, he bent over, and bought them up. While one hand held the blood in his throat, he groped around on his pants with his other. Finally, he pulled a pint bottle of whisky from his pants. He tried to break it against the bed post, but it wouldn't break. He tried against the lamp stand. Dee heard breaking glass and then saw Saucedo inching toward her with a fist full of glass shards. She swiped and poked. He swiped and poked. Dee felt like he could have just grabbed and poked and twisted the glass shards into her. But he didn't. Maybe he wanted to torture her.

She was cutting his arm. He was cutting hers. And after the girly-style swipes, he got his fist full of glass across Dee's face. She backed up and raised her hands to her face, one still holding the switchblade, not daring to let go. He still held his throat. But he smiled.

Dee heard the door rattling in its frame and then heard Charlie shout her name. "Help, Charlie," she said loud but not screaming.

Saucedo turned from her toward the door in time to see Charlie come stumbling through it. Saucedo raised a bloody fist. Charlie raised his hand. In Charlie's hand was pistol with a silencer. Charlie shot twice. Saucedo gurgled, fell over backward, and died.

Charlie stepped toward Dee and looked at her face. "Oh Jesus," he said. "Hold on."

So Dee tried to hold her face together while Charlie closed the door and flipped on the light. He looked once at Dee and breathed in. Dee pushed harder on her face. Charlie flipped the mattress over and pulled up the plastic sheets. He then folded the plastic sheets around Saucedo and then huffed as he pulled bloody Saucedo to one side of the room. He went into the bathroom and came out with wet, soapy towels. He began trying to clean up what he could with a soap and water.

In the light, with Charlie checking back over his shoulder at her, Dee realized that she was stark naked. A dancer and hooker gets used to having no clothes on so that she sometimes forgets whether she's dressed or not, especially if her face is slashed open. Dee took several steps forward and bent down to grab her clothes. While she was bent over, she saw a few drops of her blood mix with the mess on the carpet.

As she tried to stuff herself into her short skirt and tight blouse, Dee thought she ought to look in the mirror, just to check out the damage. When she got most of her clothes on, she moved toward the mirror, but Charlie said, "Don't do it. Best not to see yet."

Dee backed slowly away from the mirror, feeling her face, like she was checking to see if it was still there. Dee's mind zipped from then until years down the line to what she would do with a ruined face.

When he was satisfied with his cleaning, Charlie turned off the light, opened the door, and checked in the hall. A small, young Mexican boy pushed a rolling food serving cart into the room. Together, Charlie and the boy pushed and tugged the plastic-wrapped Saucedo onto the cart. With parts of him hanging over the sides, they rolled Saucedo to a service elevator, took him out through the kitchen, and threw him into the bed of a pickup. Dee followed behind them the whole way, holding her face. And then Charlie got in the pickup and told her to get in the Mexican boy's car.

Dee climbed into a battered Plymouth Valiant with the boy, and watched Charlie drive off with Saucedo's body. The boy began to chatter, "You don't look too good." Dee was afraid to move any part of her face for fear of it becoming all distorted. "So how was it? I mean, like what was you thinking with all that cutting going on?"

Dee just remained silent for those ten blocks to Santa Rosa Hospital Emergency Room where that Mexican boy dropped her off. When she walked in, a pregnant woman said, "Oh, my God. Honey, does it hurt?"

"It stung," Dee said. "Now it stopped."

Dee knew that the doctor and nurses knew what she was and how she got that cut as they stitched her up. After all, they worked late in an emergency room in a downtown. They had seen whores cut up and beaten up before. You just couldn't know when a john was going to get pissed off.

Just as the sun was coming up, Charlie appeared in the emergency room to pick Dee up. He hung his head to keep from looking at her. He couldn't make himself say anymore than, "Goddamn, I'm sorry." Dee asked him where the body was. "Best you don't ask," he said.

"So okay, you've done this before. What do we do now? How safe are we?"

Charlie squinted into the sun. "On the seat there is the rest of Pinky's money. Best if you just get out of town and find honest work."

Dee nodded to herself because she didn't really want to stick around anyway. San Antonio, for her, was as dead as Saucedo. Still Charlie looked like he was going to cry. "It's just that I'm going to really miss you," he said.

* * *

That cut on her face turned into a forked scar across her forehead and left cheek. So she slid a rung or two down the whore ladder. She also did some stripping, and she managed strip joints in Oklahoma City, which of course has the reputation of having the best titty-bars in the country out on West I-40. The whoring and titty bar work was mostly for getting by.

She was not about to spend Pinky's money on getting by. She invested in savings accounts, stocks, bonds, certificates of deposit and watched that money grow. When she would tell us about looking into a whore's eyes to see if she had lost her soul, she'd add that the question was really when and how she lost her soul. The *why* was usually obvious. Then she'd smile, point up at the scar on her forehead, and say she was not a true whore, just a getting-by whore. She'd smile real big and say she still had her soul.

Eventually Dee drifted with the oil booms and oil shows to Odessa, where she made friends quick. On a strict schedule she made out herself, she visited all the bars, so she met those of us who worked with bars, whores, or titty joints. Dee got back to Texas after 1971 when Texas left its dark age behind and voted in liquor by the drink at county option. So Texans left their bottles and the paper bags they wrapped them in at home. Now, if the Baptist and Church or Christ didn't completely take over the county, you could pay a bartender in a restaurant or bar with a liquor license to mix you a drink. For those like us, we thought there ought to be a state-wide holiday commemorating this bill. But most of us, out in West Odessa, couldn't afford the liquor license, so we still sold set ups and beers and passed out paper bags.

Dee learned a lot from sitting in our bars. With her looks spoiled, Dee found that she had a talent for organization, so she ran whores. Dee started her day in the early afternoon by making the rounds at the bars out in dusty, unincorporated West Odessa with its trailers, convenience stores, and pipelines. During the late seventies early eighties boom, some people were even living in tents out in West Odessa. She recruited girls and customers. And for two hours a day, late in the afternoon, she would sit in one bar and take calls. A gentleman would call, and she would arrange for a date. She changed the bars, and so she changed the numbers. That way she avoided the police and got to know us all.

She saw the country girls who drifted in, saw their desperation in the way they stood, like they had realized they weren't going to find some upstanding, well-to-do Christian man. So she recruited them. And she would counsel them. She would tell them they could make good, quick, money, but she would caution them about losing their souls or their looks if they stayed in too long or used their money for drugs or booze instead of investments.

And when the big International Oil Shows were held every other year, Dee made contacts with corporate executives and got dates for them. Then she bought a duplex right in the middle of The First Quality Motel, which was just off Second Street. She decorated it in gold and red with red shag carpet to give it a whorehouse look, and used that duplex as her head-quarters. During the oil show, young whores from all over the country, some from Mexico and Asia, roamed the street parallel to Second. They needed a place to take their clients. So Dee was there ahead of them organizing, advising, taking a cut. She and her whores made enough to live comfortable for a whole year during the two-week long oil shows. And all the while, Dee had Pinky's money sitting and growing.

And after a late-seventies oil show, to celebrate, Dee was sitting in the Tank—an upscale restaurant and bar, which was really a holding tank bored out on the inside with some windows and doors added and turned into a restaurant and bar—when a handsome man in a cashmere sport-coat, tropical wool dress slacks, and Bass Wejuns loafers asked if he could sit down with her. Dee of course thought this was the usual ploy. "I'm not working," she said.

"Neither am I," the man said. "You're alone. I'm alone. You look interesting." He shrugged and held up his hands.

"You mean the scar?" Dee said.

"I mean all of you," he said.

"Don't bullshit me. I got that scar from a whiskey bottle."

"Don't get pissed off at me. I didn't swing the bottle at you."

Dee liked this conversation no matter where it was leading because it was different from the others she got from men. So she let this man buy her drink, then another, and another.

Then they ate. They gorged on steaks. Because the oil show was over and the visitors gone and most locals just tired out, the place emptied out. So Dee and this lively fella went to other bars, seedier bars, real Odessa bars, with gravel parking lots, no liquor license, ugly strippers, and maybe a whore down for the oil show but still stuck in town. Everyone knew Dee, and everyone knew the gentleman with her. We whispered to each other about this odd couple. In the parking lot of one such bar, Dee climbed into this man's convertible Mustang, leaned across the console and kissed him. After they went to Dee's place and had some clumsy, fumbling sex, Danny

Fowler told Dee he was gay.

Of course, we all knew Danny Fowler was queer. That's why we whispered with each other when we saw him and Dee out together. We knew that he would cruise around in that convertible, spending his Mama's money, looking for a wayward oil field worker who didn't quite fit in, wasn't quite sure of himself, was hiding a secret too. But we mostly liked him, and so did Dee. They became fast friends.

But it was almost like Saucedo was not dead yet, for trouble caught up with Dee. She was just marked for it. After a shower, she felt a lump. So then there was the trip to the doctor, the diagnosis, the choices, the mastectomy, and then the chemo and radiation. But she had no insurance. Women who run whores don't qualify for group rates. She figured she was healthy, figured that insurance was the one thing that she could omit, so she didn't bother. The bills stacked up. Pinky's money was gone. Saucedo was back.

So Danny Fowler took her to a nice meal at the Tank with his mother. Dee and Mina Fowler, daughter of old ranch money made way-wealthy by oil, just eyed each other. And some witnesses claimed Dee risked everything by saying, "Well, we going to fight or fuck?"

Mina came right back, "I thought this was about money, not fucking or fighting."

But somehow the two tough women sized each other up and liked what they saw. Mina probably saw that, for whatever reason, Dee made Danny happy, so Danny got his mother to pay for the rest of Dee's treatment. Stories like that make you want to cry.

Dee was sort of proud of the outcome too. That's when, sometimes, to amuse those of us who knew her and to shock those who didn't, she'd pull down her blouse and bra show us where her breast used to be. Dee was somehow proud of her mangled feminine beauty and liked to show off her matching scars: the one on her forehead and the one on her chest.

Naturally then, during the 1981 Odessa Oil Show, when the Ector County sheriff's deputies found, Danny Fowler's body dumped in a ditch, missing a Bass Wejun, his camelhair sportcoat curled around one arm, Dee took it hard. Most of us knew Danny liked to "cruise" around town looking for what he shouldn't find. Most, when we admitted to each other, knew that urge, only poor Danny's was pointed in the wrong direction at the wrong gender. So we knew, with his several trips to jail, his several ass kickings, Danny was risking a big, big bruising; only we never thought it would get him killed.

Dee knew more than us. She knew more than she let on to the police and the sheriff's department. She told half of what she knew to that young Ector County Deputy, Justin Brady, eager to make a name for himself, and so sent him off chasing his tail. The cops needed proof to get the truth; Dee didn't. So she started her own investigation. She started with a trip to Mina Fowler's ranch to get financing for her investigation.

Mina Fowler's ranch straddled the Ector and Crane County line. Her ranching family had some money but didn't become really wealthy until oil started sprouting out of the ranch. For old time's sake, she still kept some decorative cattle. She collected husbands then kicked them off the ranch until only she and Danny were at the ranch. We never knew why she stayed other than she just wanted to be on the property her grandfather made prosper. We never knew why Danny stayed instead of going somewhere where they might look the other way while he followed his misdirected urges. Maybe, whatever his urges, he was a part of West Texas too.

Inside Mina Fowler's ranch house, Dee just couldn't help looking around to see how her social betters lived. She calculated just what she would have to do and how much she would have to make to live in a place like Mina's. While she noted, Mina sloshed the vodka out of her wine glass and led Dee to her red leather sofa. They sat at opposite ends.

"We meet again," Mina said to Dee to start the conversation.

Dee didn't wait, "So you know me and what I do."

"I even know where you do it: The First Quality Motel."

"The point is I'm used to being on both sides of the law. So far, I've been paddling in mid-river, and I'm hoping you can help me decide what to do."

Mina raised her wine glass to her lips and sipped her mid-morning vodka. "I suppose this has to do with my son?"

"Yes."

Before Dee could go on Mina interrupted, "So does everybody know what happened?"

"I witnessed part of what happened, and I told what I saw to the cops. But I didn't tell them what I know."

Mina pulled her head back as though to focus on Dee. "So what do you know?"

"Several months ago, Jennifer Peveto came here from Seminole, Texas with the sole intention of getting fast money. I cleaned her up a little and helped her learn her trade. She now calls herself Buffy St. Cloud. She still has a lot to learn. But the last time I knew Danny was alive, he was in his convertible with two other boys, and Danny bought those two boys a good time, which was Buffy St. Cloud. Buffy took them to one of the First Quality Motel rooms. She left them. The next morning, the room had some splatters of blood, and Ector County Sheriff's deputies found Danny's body in a ditch."

Mina squirmed in her seat and looked like she was going to fall back into her daily crying. "And do you know who did it?"

"I have a pretty good idea, and Buffy St. Cloud thinks that she can identify them."

"Have you told the police?"

"No."

Mina shakily stood. "So you know why Danny was with those boys and why they killed him?"

"Yes. Of course, I do. We both know. Jennifer says from what she heard, these two youngish boys met Danny at the Tank. It is his usual haunt. The place he starts his night."

Mina looked out a window at her decorative cows. "He has a history of that. Sometimes he gets lucky. Sometimes, they find out what he is afterwards; then they beat the shit out of him. I've made a habit of bailing him out."

"Like I said, I've had some experience in these things. My guess is that these two guys knew exactly what Danny was. They knew exactly what he would do. So they played the part. They even got a piece of Jennifer's Peveto ass. Now you think about it. You think. Danny's car is gone. Nobody's found his billfold. My guess is that they set him up. Once Jennifer left, they beat the shit out of him, stole his money, then fenced his car."

"So it wasn't because he was homosexual." Mina looked almost relieved.

"I let the cops believe that. The whole thing just seems more planned."

"But you know what it will look like? You know what the cops will tell the press and the prosecuting attorney."

"So you're not cooperating with the cops. In fact, you've told them to just drop the case."

"I don't want that information in the papers. I don't want to advertise what Danny did."

"I guess that's your choice. It's not his."

Mina got up to refresh her drink, but on her way, she turned around and wobbled a little on her high boot heels. "Easy for you to say, especially from where you came from."

Dee stood and took a step to be face to face with Mina and as tall. "You don't know where I came from or what I'm suggesting."

"I don't want the police involved. I don't want any more people to know."

"Do you want the boys that killed him punished?"

"Yes." Mina said and raised her drink.

"How bad?"

"I gave you a large sum of money once."

"If I can do this, and there is no guarantee, then I want the same amount."

Mina took a tentative step forward. "What do you intend to do?"

"I don't know that I should tell you."

"Then I'll commit. I want those two boys dead."

"Okay," Dee said.

* * *

So instead of Charlie Brodsky, Dee worked with Jennifer Peveto or Buffy St. Cloud. Jennifer was actually a skinny little girl just over twenty with no particular savvy or looks, so Dee had coached her on how to become Buffy St. Cloud. But Jennifer had a good memory: one of the boys with Danny had on a cowboy hat; the other was little older; and they both worked on a casing crew. The Oil Show was about to leave town, customers would be dropping off. So Dee hurried, she hung out in the bars during the days and asked questions about who knew what. She found out what Jennifer told her.

In a West Odessa bar, she heard a guy talking about this Barry guy and a friend of his who came in drunk when the bar opened for the 7:30 a.m. crowd just getting off a shift. They talked about this red convertible Mustang they had sold to a Mexican who was going to paint it and drive it to Mexico. The next night, a bartender told her that Barry had come in alone and talked about getting a whore. Dee told the bartender that, if he saw Barry, to contact her. The next night, the bartender gave Dee a slip of paper with a phone number on it. Dee phoned Barry and suggested he and Jennifer reunite. She told him where she would be.

Dee and Jennifer rehearsed and prepared. Dee called Mina. And then Barry pulled up to Jennifer as she was parading her goods down a street parallel to Second Street. "Thought I'd find you here," the voice under a gimme cap said.

"Where's your friend from out of town?" Jennifer remembered to ask.

"He's left town?"

"Why?" Jennifer asked.

"His business," his buddy said.

"Where did he go?"

"Don't know."

"Are you Barry?"

"I don't remember giving my name."

Jennifer stumbled, "But you told my manager Dee your name." Jennifer got by with the slip so then she shifted the conversation, "I bet you remember my name."

"I couldn't forget Buffy St. Cloud."

And Jennifer showed her friend to the First Quality Motel, just as she had done when she had first seen him. And then they parked in front of Dee's duplex. When they walked in the door, simple, skinny Jennifer gave Dee the "hi" sign they had rehearsed. Dee handed her the key to number three and asked, "Are you sure?" Jennifer looked quickly at Barry, frowned, then just barely nodded her head.

Dee asked them to wait, said she had to straighten out the room. So she ran ahead, let herself in, stepped into the closet, and pulled the door shut. In the dark, Dee debated just one last time about what she was going to do. She tried to see far enough into the future to know what this act might lead to. But her mind drifted back to Danny and his indignity and hers. Dee was wiser now. She knew what she would do with the money. So she waited.

Dee heard the door to the motel open, heard the click of a light, saw a band of light at her feet, leaned against the side of the closet and tried not to breathe.

After dancing naked in front of Barry, after warming him up so to speak, Jennifer asked if they couldn't please, this time turn off the lights because she wanted things to be sweet and romantic and because he, Barry, was special. Jennifer cooed, and though Dee couldn't see her, Dee knew that smartened-up Jennifer dropped her head but lifted her eyes to beg Barry. So the lights went off.

And then there were grunts and groans and Jennifer screaming with fake delight. Then Jennifer asked if she couldn't please get on top. "What, what," Barry said. "Why you so particular?"

"Ain't you getting your money's worth?" Jennifer asked.

"That's better," Jennifer cooed some more. And then Dee slowly pushed the closet door open. She took a tentative step toward the bed and saw Barry's head pointing back at her from the foot of the bed. Jennifer had maneuvered him just as they had planned. With two quick steps, Dee was to the foot of the bed and Barry's head.

"Hey, there's somebody in here?" Barry asked as he pulled his eyes from Jennifer and up toward the tops of their sockets.

"Baby, Baby, Baby," Jennifer said and looked through the dark for Dee. And Barry lifted his chin and tilted his head back on to his crown to try to see behind him.

"What the hell," Barry said when Jennifer froze. As he tried to flip Jennifer off him, Dee pulled the switchblade across his throat, just like it was a cantaloupe with the rind peeled away. A neat line of blood spread under his chin and began to trickle.

Jennifer stuck her knuckles in her mouth to keep from screaming and jumped off Barry. She hopped up and down and rapidly waved her hands in front of her over the thought of screwing a bleeding man. Barry's head tilted back some more, making the thin line under his chin wider, and his eyes looked at Dee. "If you're still alive, then know that this if for Danny Fowler. You shouldn't have set him up," Dee said. Barry gurgled. "I bet it don't seem like you got very much from him now."

Jennifer ran to the front door and turned on the light. The slit in his throat had tributaries of blood coming out of it. Dee looked down Barry's body: his hairless chest, his shrinking male equipment, his socks. "Why do they always leave their socks on? Where's he going to run? And from who?" Dee asked.

Then Dee and naked Jennifer reached under the mattress and pulled the plastic sheet off the bed with Barry's body still on it. They bundled up sheet, clothes, Barry, and Jennifer's clothes in the plastic sheet. Jennifer changed into a pair jeans and a t-shirt that they had stashed in a drawer, and she and Dee strained to flip the lump of body and bed clothes on to a plastic and aluminum lawn recliner they pulled from under the bed. Then they got the lawn recliner to Dee's pickup.

They drove out to the Fowler ranch and met Mina. Mina had had a ranch hand bulldoze a ditch that morning. Mina even helped them pull the evidence into a ditch. They sprinkled gas on it and set it afire. While the fire was roaring, Dee showed Barry's billfold to Mina and then threw it into the fire. The next morning, Mina said she would get the same ranch hand who bulldozed the ditch to cover up the charred parts. And then Mina gave both Jennifer and Dee envelopes loaded with cash.

After some late night phone calls and some crying, Jennifer got over everything and disappeared. But Dee stayed. Dee was smart. She knew that, with the Baptists, the Church of Christers, and the other Turbo-Christians complaining to the police department, the cops would eventually shut her down. So that's when she diversified by buying bars and vending machines. With her profits, she bought more. When the boom busted and the money was all pissed away, Dee made even more money. She even suffered through several shootings in her bars and one killing.

Over the years, if you regularly ran across her and if you really got to know her and if she really wanted to impress you that she was just as tough as any man and if she really trusted you, she'd tell her story about slitting two men's throats. Surely, some of the cops even came to know her story. Of those of us who have heard her story, nobody says Barry or Saucedo deserved it. But then nobody really believes Danny Fowler deserved it either. But things work out in their twisted way. But most of all, none of us can blame Dee for nothing. We consider Dee one of us. She may have been a whore, but she kept her soul.

Pissed Away

My father steps out the backdoor of the Cactus Lounge and into an early morning breeze. The sun is just coming up, and it lights a pumpjack. To somebody not from West Texas, the pumpjack looks like a giant mosquito sucking up blood from the earth. The line of orange the rising sun makes and the glitter from the new pumpjack almost make the morning pretty, but the cool, kind summer breeze, not a rough West Texas spring wind, blows tumbleweeds and trash against the pumpjack and a barbed wire fence farther away in the half-light.

My father squats on the steps, the way an old farmer would, looks down, and sees crumpled laundry at the bottom of the steps. Raising himself, my father toes the laundry and hears a grumble and notices the laundry shifting. One of the drunk gamblers at Snake Popp's game must have come outside while it was still dark, maybe to piss, fallen, and then passed out. Best to let him lie, my father thinks, and squats back down on the step. His head hurts. His eyes still water from all the smoke inside the Cactus Lounge. He coughs up some goo from his burning throat and lungs. His clothes smell from the smoke. He has just closed up another one of Snake's invitation-only gambling nights. Amarillo Slim himself had spent the night in the Cactus Lounge, losing big and leaving well before sunrise. Snake had several tables set up and different games went on at each.

My father is Snake Popp's "assistant." My father is not tall, but he is a good two hundred and ten pounds. His is squat like a pulling guard or a bulldog. He is the type of guy that a troublemaker can look at and think he might be able to whip but wouldn't want to try. My father's face tells a troublemaker that he would have to pay for starting any shit. So Snake hires my father to keep peace.

All night, with Johnny Dexter, his partner, my father had watched over the card players. The pros stayed sober and concentrated on the cards. Amateurs faked laughing at their losings or went outside and cried about them. The lump of laundry at my father's feet was probably a crier.

My father and Johnny Dexter watched them all. Somebody could have just lost control of his nerves. Somebody could have gotten pissed. So my father and Johnny just watched. At the end of the night, the way Snake Popp pushed his shoulders back, my father knew Snake Popp had won big.

Snake Popp is mostly a legitimate business man. He is not nicknamed Snake because he is as mean as a snake but because when he was just kid, he was bitten by a rattler and lost a chunk of skin off his ankle. Snake grew up liking to show that scar to people. So he became "Snake," and then he became fairly rich.

The backdoor hits my father in the back. He looks up and sees Dee Price in the doorframe. Dee owns the building and the rights to the vending machines. Betty Howard's husband owned the business, but he died, and now, to support herself, Betty runs the bar. So Dee, trying to help Betty, being a friend of Snake's, arranged for the game after midnight closing. "Almost pretty, isn't it?" Dee says and sits beside my father.

Her body is taut. She has lost a breast to cancer and likes to tell people about the operation. She even likes to show them her scar. Her hair is swept back from her face in wings, as is the fashion; so she is attractive. But a forked scar running down her forehead to her left cheek ruins her face. As with her mastectomy, she likes to tell people about that scar. A broken whiskey bottle gave it to her. My father looks at the bobbing pumpjack to avoid Dee because she wants him to work for her. "Long night," she says.

"It's what Snake pays me for."

"There's better money and shorter hours," Dee says. "If you want them."

My father looks at the trash lined up on the fences and watches a tumbleweed catch on the pumpjack and then roll away. Far off in a small pasture a frisky young horse trots the length of the fence and then back again, just burning off his energy. "You're right. It is almost pretty."

The few clouds in the sky have pink undersides. A rooster crows. There is the smell of rain on the wind, though my father knows that it will not rain this Sunday. And it is as cool as it will be all day. He watches because this truly is as beautiful as it gets in West Odessa, the unincorporated, ill-planned community of trailers, cinderblock buildings, and small bars out west of Odessa. And in just a moment, as it happens in West

Texas, the sun pulls itself above the flat horizon and suddenly the morning is bright yellow light and hot.

It is 1984, the boom has busted, the locals have pissed away the money that they made. As the plaques in bars say: "An Oil Field Prayer: Please Lord, give us another boom, and I promise not to piss this one away." But there is still gambling and bootlegging in dry counties and illegal girls from Mexico stripping in the Stampede Club, so Snake Popp is still making a living even if people can't always pay him. So Snake Popp hires my father and Johnny Dexter. And Dee, recognizing a tough, intimidating man when she sees him, wants to hire my father too. "If you can tear yourself away from the view, Colton, Snake wants to see you."

As my father pushes himself up, Dee says, "You know with just a little more nerve, you could be making more money than what Snake pays you."

"I ain't gone to jail for what Snake has me do."

"No yet," Dee says. "So are you making what you should for what you are risking?"

"I'm making due," my father says.

My father walks into the haze of cigarette and cigar smoke in the Cactus Lounge. Next to the bar, with his head on his folded arms and his snoring rattling the rickety bar and a glass, is Johnny Dexter, my father's partner. My father walks up to the barstool and lightly kicks it. Johnny doesn't budge. My father kicks it again. Johnny pulls his head up and shakes it. "Don't let Snake see you sleeping this soon after working," my father says. Johnny is much younger than my father. He is bigger but not as scary. He has a gentle look in his hangdog face and eyes. People might not think he will do what he threatens to do to them. They know my father would do what he threatens to do them. But Johnny is quick; he tries hard; and he listens to my father.

The Cactus Lounge has an office, and my father enters it without knocking. He sits across from the card table that serves as a desk. Snake comes out of another door that connects to the bar. He slaps cologne on his face, trying to wake up. Snake's silver hair is combed straight back, making him look like that ol' country singer Porter Wagoner. Snake makes it a habit, even in these hot summer months, to never look hot. He makes his living with his big, fancy bar, his bootlegging in dry counties, and at his stripper bar. But his passion is gambling. All his businesses and passions require that you bluff, but Snake wants no one to know when he is bluffing, including my father.

"Job well done," he says to my father. "Went real smooth tonight. Course there was some weeping and gnashing of teeth, but nobody just lost their shit."

"Dee's offered me another job," my father says.

"Now, Colton," Snake says. "I'm being as fair to you as I can. But this bust has busted more than the oil companies. Without roughnecks fucking around and throwing their money away, I ain't got the profits I used to."

"I got a family," my father says.

"That Mexican family you married into still eating up your money?"

"I got expenses."

"And just what you think you're going to do with your talents other than to work for me? You think that family of yours is going help you climb up the social register? You think you going to join First Baptist and go to church?"

Snake, in his polo shirt with the little horse figure where the pocket should be, combs his hair back up over his head, shakes his comb, and puts it back into his cotton slacks' back pocket. "Dee's talking shit. What can she offer you? Picking up and servicing vending machines? Throwing out drunks?"

"I think it's more along the lines of what I do now."

"And so there you go, you admit it. You got it pretty easy."

"I'm fixing to go home. Like you, I been up all night."

"Dee and I both got a problem with a deadbeat. Don Smiley owes me some money from our little games, and he owes Dee some rent. Neither one of us likes to call the police or the county. So we need you and Johnny to pay a visit."

"So I am working for Dee."

"See there, you get what you wish for," Snake says. "Dee and me go back." Snake smiles. He has worked on his suntan by sitting out at his pool two hours a day. He is lean from swimming in that pool. He has a thin silver moustache to match his silver hair. His slacks are white. His polo shirt is purple, and he looks as fresh as if he has just gotten up, showered, shaved, and dressed. "Listen, let's not get bitchy here. Why don't you let me buy you breakfast?"

"I got to get home."

"Got or want to get home?"

"My family's going to be in church, and I'm supposed to watch my two boys."

"We can still get breakfast."

"Maybe, Johnny'll go."

"This family business is twisting your stomach and your brain in knots. Relax a little." Snake pats my father's shoulder as he walks out the office door. A year before, my father and Johnny drove to El Paso and checked into a Holiday Inn. Then they went to a liquor store just outside of town and started carrying cases out of the store and into their car. It was payment for Snake. A month before, someone started saying nasty things to one of the strippers at the Stampede. Then he tried to follow her home. She didn't speak English, but she made Snake and my father understand. When that lonely man told my father and Johnny to fuck off, my father plowed straight into him, pinning him against the wall, and kneed him in the crotch. While Johnny pounded him, my father took off that man's thick belt and wrapped it over his knuckles, so his knuckles wouldn't get so battered. After pounding him with that belt, my father looked at his battered knuckles. It was a money belt with a zipper on its inside. So my father kept it and gave it to Snake.

My father steps into the Cactus Lounge and the slanting sunbeams filled with the dust falling down from the ceiling and the smoke wafting about. Snake comes out behind him and yells to Johnny, "Hey, Johnny boy, your partner don't want none, but you interested in breakfast?"

Johnny's face brightens up, and he looks at my father, "Boss is buying breakfast and you refuse?" he says to my father.

"Go on ahead. I got family to tend to," my father says. Johnny jumps off his barstool. Smiling, the new morning sun gleaming off his silver hair, Snake steers himself out of the Cactus Lounge, and Johnny Dexter, with one last look over his shoulder at my father, follows Snake into the sunshine.

My father steps through several sunbeams when Dee comes in from the backdoor. "That fella you saw outside got sober enough to stagger down the road. He can't remember where he left his car."

My father plants his elbows on the bar and worries. "Maybe if you'd've studied harder in high school and gone to college, you'd be doing the books for Snake instead busting heads," Dee tells him.

"I was never good with numbers," my father says.

"So you don't know what adds up to what," Dee says, and my father smiles. "You want a drink? I'm buying," Dee says.

"I got to go home," my father says.

"You know," Dee says, "I got a friend. Ol' Bill Sears. He sells old, beat-up cars to illegal Mexicans. He knows they're poor, knows they can't make the payments, but he sells them, collects what he can for several months, takes a loss several months, then repos it. When he has a night off and needs cash, your partner, Johnny, rides shotgun for Bill's repo guys. Then Bill sells that car again, and again, and again. The oil bust has been good for Bill. I'm thinking of going into business with Bill Sears. Why not you?"

"Why you so interested in me?"

Dee pours herself a shot and sips it. "I don't like to see people sell themselves short."

Who knows why Dee wants to help my father. Maybe good, reliable people who provide the type of help my father does are hard to come by. So my father goes to breakfast with her instead of Snake and Johnny and listens to her schemes and scams.

* * *

My father lives with his family and on and off with his in-laws in a small house on Adams Street. The house is old and will probably soon just crumble, but it is cheap. My father knows that he wants a family. He knows that a family in place in a house is a part of what you are supposed to want, a part of social and economic advancement. But he hasn't prepared for a family, a house, or advancement.

He comes home to a nearly empty house. In the kitchen, his father-in-law, Raul, sits and listens to a throbbing Norteño song. It is about bleeding and broken hearts and the women who cause them. "We have TV," my father says.

"I like the radio better," Raul says.

"So they've already gone to church?" my father asks.

"Early mass," Raul says. "And you?"

"I done fine my whole life without the church. It's for women anyway. Besides, I watch the boys now."

My father leaves my grandfather to his coffee and music and walks down the hall to the last bedroom. He opens the door and steps in to see his sons. They are both in their pajamas and still sleepy because they have gotten up even earlier than on a school day. The older one watches some show about animals on TV. He looks up and smiles at his father. The younger one just keeps smearing deep blue across the coarse page of his coloring book and does not look up. "You boys, not going to say *hello* to your Daddy," my father says.

And in unison, the boys say, "Hi, Daddy."

My father scoops up his younger son and then presses him up in the air until he almost touches the ceiling. This is me he picks up. I have lost amusement with the games that he plays with me and my brother. I see more of my grandfather and various uncles than I do of my father, and they play better games. So *father* to me is this shapeless term for the man who I know is responsible for the food, order, and money. Like food, order, and money, my father has a distant relation to me. I know that these things exist, that they are important, that they account for my life as it is. But I have no direct connection to any of them, only several old games, like the airplane ride under the ceiling. I stretch out my arms and hum as my father taught me.

My brother, Arnie, is interested only in his TV show. He has started school and has learned to read. I am waiting to start in another month or two and am both scared and anxious of being away from my house for the biggest portion of my conscious day.

What I don't know is that my father feels just like I do. He is not sure of his relation to me or the family. He knows that he should provide money, food, and order, and he tries to do that, but he can't really see the results of what he provides. My mother runs the house. And what she can't do, Raul usually does. He doesn't know how to play with his kids. All he knows for sure is that they need more.

So we both know that we come from the same blood, that we are surrounded by the same people, that we both desire good for that group of people. But we aren't sure of much else. When my father puts me down, he knows that he does not know me or my brother.

My father leaves us and goes into his kitchen and pours himself another cup of coffee. He has already had a breakfast and coffee with Dee, so though he is tired, he knows that he cannot go to sleep. He listens to my grandfather's sad songs that he cannot understand and stares into his cup. "A man's job is his job," my grandfather says. "So you don't got to worry when you come home."

"I've been offered another job," my father says. Raul twists in his seat and reaches up to turn down the volume of his radio. "There's some things about it that are, are, are not quite right."

"You mean legal," my grandfather says. "I'm a Mexican. I know about these things. You got to figure out the risks. You got to figure what you got to lose."

"So you tell me. What have I got to lose?"

Raul turns the radio down lower. "What you mean?"

"I don't know nothing about this."

"What's this?"

"This family thing. All that goes on here."

"What's to know? Same as church. The women go. They take care of family. Your job is your job."

"But I don't know what goes on here."

"So don't."

"I got to live here."

"So live here, but don't think so much."

"So what if I was to go to jail, or get shot, or something?"

"My father swam across a river and pulled me after him. You takes your chances when you do what you got to."

Frustrated, my father stares into his coffee. His nerves dance and tingle because he wants to be in bed and well on his way to sleep. But he knows the coffee and his thinking will keep his brain sizzling. He walks through his house and looks at the crucifixes and paintings of the Virgin Mary, the brightly colored walls that Raul painted, the bare carpet. He opens the door and smiles again at his boys. He goes to his living room, turns on the TV, watches *Meet the Press* until the boring politicians and the political analysts cool his brain, and he goes to sleep.

His own snoring wakes him, and then he leaves the hum of many voices speaking Spanish. He goes into the kitchen to see children and in-laws coming into his house. The women busy themselves in his kitchen. His sons come running out, still in their pajamas, to play with their cousins. He has no idea of how many people fill his house. He has no idea if he even knows them all. Soon, grease is popping; the smell of garlic fills the air, and the kitchen warms from heating the dishes that his in-laws have brought over.

My father goes into the backyard, and the in-laws and friends are there too. He does finally recognize my mother. She is small and petite—just over five feet. She can disappear into a crowd, yet when you pick her out within a crowd, you see her distinctly, and your eyes stick on her. Likewise, her eyes can hold you in place. My father smiles, and she gives the smile back to him. But behind her smile is a look that says she is happy with her family but disappointed with my father. He walks to her and kisses her forehead, and as he does, my father hazily wishes and waits.

* * *

After two years, I walked away from my courses at Odessa Community College. I was not yet twenty-one and bored. I didn't know what I wanted to do; mostly, I just didn't want to do anything. So I lived in a one room apartment in south Odessa and smoked pot. My mother and my grandfather couldn't get too pissed off at me because, compared to my older brother, Arnie, who was in prison, I looked like the good son. My mother then came to me and said that she had a note directly from my father. I hadn't seen or spoken to my father for fifteen years, but like the voice of God, he was speaking to me through my mother via the U.S. Postal Service. My mother gave me a note with phone numbers on it. One had the name *Snake Popp* written above it in my mother's careful, looping script. The other had *Dee Price* written above it.

I called Snake Popp and, early on a spring afternoon, I walked out of the wild spring wind and into his new nightclub, the Midnight Rodeo, a cavernous, classy bar. The soles of my boots clicked as I crossed the wooden dance floor of his deserted bar to get to the office door. A bartender warily watched me. I knocked, and a voice told me to come in.

I opened the door to silver-haired Snake sitting behind his desk. "So you're Colton's boy?"

I nodded and sat down in front of his desk when he motioned. He chewed gum in one side of his mouth. "This stuff is supposed to make you quit smoking," he said and chomped. He ran one hand through his silver hair. "Why do you suppose Colton sent you to me?"

"To get a job. I'm kind of down on my luck."

"You don't want the kind of jobs I got," he said.

"I don't think I got the right to be picky."

"I got nothing where you do something romantic like bartending."

"I need a job," I said.

Snake pushed himself up from his chair. His silver hair matched his silver slacks. He ran his hands through his hair again and left two indentations right at the top sides of his head. His mouth worked grinding the gum. "You been in many fights?"

"Few."

"Colton, Colton," Snake said and shook his head. With his head still hanging, he said, "Look, truth is, I just got nothing." I nodded. "No, truth is I got nothing I want to give you." I nodded. "You catching my drift?" I nodded again.

Snake sat back down in his chair and put his feet upon his desk. "Your father should have thought of that," he said.

"I think he did," I said.

"No, no. You run on and find someone else willing to give you what you shouldn't have. The old days are gone."

"I need a job," I said.

"Did your father say you should go see Dee Price?"

"Yes sir."

"Well then you go see her. I owe your father, but your father don't know Dee and me don't associate much anymore. Best of luck to you."

I went to the Cactus Lounge, where Dee had an office. She greeted me and said she had been expecting me. "So you talked with my father?"

"Off and on. Mostly off. Nobody from the old days talks much to your father," she said. "So you need a job."

"How did you know?"

"I talk on and off to Snake Popp."

"What kind of work are you willing to do?"

"The kind that pays," I said.

I had better luck with Dee. She started me out cleaning, picking up, and hauling. Sometimes, on weekends, I rode shotgun on a repo truck. While some guy named Larry backed up the truck to a parked car and attached it, I'd sit in the cab with a shotgun. My instructions were to fire in the air if anybody tried to stop Larry. Only if I saw a gun pointed directly at Larry was I to aim and pull the trigger. Then Dee moved me up to collecting the coins from the vending machines. Since I was out late at night with bags of coins, she gave me a pistol and told me to be careful with it but not to take chances.

And when I had the time, I would sometimes drop into the Cactus Lounge and have a beer with her even though, at first, I was just shy of twenty-one. And sometimes, I went into one of the other bars she owned: the Silver Stallion, the Mustang, the Post, the Office. And when she felt like it, she told me about my father when she first met him. She told me about Johnny Dexter. Then she told me that I could never replace my father, but that I could become another Johnny Dexter.

After a year and half, just-turned twenty-one and thus a legal adult with a job, a car, and a gun, I felt good about myself. To my mother and grandfather, I was at least supporting myself. To Dee, as she often said, I had a future, but I was still kind of hazy about my future. On a cold day, with the chilly wind outside the Cactus Lounge but with some still finding its way into the bar and some still shaking the walls from the outside, I had just dropped off some deposits from coins and was sitting at a table, having a beer, reviewing my life or what there was of it when Dee walked out of the office with a short, mean looking man. He had a scar across the bridge of his nose that almost matched Dee's scar. "Michael," Dee said. "This is your father."

Dee turned back to her office, and with the wind whistling through the walls and the frames of the windows, my father stepped toward me, his hands in his jacket, scaring me because I thought he might pull those hands out and beat the hell out of me. "Good to see you," he said. And then a smile cracked his face. "You changed," he said.

He sat down across from me. I saw myself. He was short and squat, just like me. But he was wide, and even with a jacket and fedora on, he looked like he was muscular. His face was not quite like mine but all angles, with scars, and baked to a dark brown. He was Anglo, yet he was darker than I was, and I was half Mexican. His lids seemed permanently draped over half his eyes. Under his eyes, his cheeks were puffy. He was man who could do some damage to you. His face told you that he wouldn't mind damaging you.

"I got a rented Lincoln Continental outside. You want to take a drive around town while I reminisce?"

I just said "sure."

His face lit up as he drove around town and passed his old haunts. He told me about fights, about who he beat up, about close scrapes. He told me about Snake: good enough man and tough as they come on the gambling table, but a real "pussy" in an actual fight, which was why he had hired my father and Johnny Dexter. Then he drove by the house on Adams Street that I barely remembered. Then we drove by the house where my mother and her new husband and my grandfather now lived. "Who you think bought that house for them?" he asked me. I didn't have to have answer.

Then we drove through the wind and the blowing trash and tumble-weeds and dust back to the Cactus Lounge. Some of the dust, wind, and trash followed us in, and my father sat at a table and put a pint bottle of bourbon on the table, and a young waitress bought us coke and ice. Dee was gone. So my father got to the point. "You see what I got. You seen that car outside. I own one just like it. In Dallas, I got a nicer house than your mama, and I live in it alone. You understand me, boy?"

"Yes," I lied.

My father slammed the table with his flat palm. "No you don't. That was set up, testing your honesty. You don't know shit. Ain't no way I can be a father to you. Not now. I'm just this old guy with some money attached to him. But you looked at my face. Dee probably told you some things. I explained some things I done. And now I'm telling you, you stick with Dee, and you can have what I got."

"Yes sir, I'm working at it," I said.

"You ain't listening, Michael. You think. You want what I got?"

"Yes."

"No."

"All right, no.'"

"That's right. I'm just this old guy with some money. So I will deposit money in an account for you for you to get your ass back in college and erase the bad mark you left there."

"But I got this."

"But you don't listen." He lifted his bottle and took a sip. "You seen that scar on Dee's face? She shown you that scar on her chest where they cut off a tit?" He didn't wait for me to answer, but the answer was that I hadn't seen her chest. "She likes to show off that surgery. Makes her think she's tough. Well, she is tough. And she'll make you tough. And tough can be useful to some people with money. And you can be living in a big house by yourself, driving a Lincoln Continental, and chewing on your own liver because you know all you got is nothing, is just the price somebody paid for you, and now they own your sorry ass. And there's your brother in prison eating his liver because he knows he made his life into total shit. And here you are flunking out of college and pissing away anything you got."

I was getting scared. "You ain't going to hit me are you?"

My father started laughing. "No, beating you ain't going to do no good. You ain't listening. I'm telling you I'll pay for you to get your ass back in college and then out of it and make less money than me and end up with a shitty little house and some screaming kids of your own because you got a job some college asshole can get. And that ain't the place where this job is leading."

"I don't get it," I admitted.

My father reached into his jacket and pulled out a check. He put it in front of me. "You get one of these a year for three years. You can piss it all away. Or you can invest it by giving yourself a glimpse of a different type a world than this and seeing if you like it better. Dee will be here awhile."

I couldn't believe the amount written on the check. "How did you get this kind of money?"

My father stuck his forefinger up under the brim of his hat and pushed up, so I could see his mangled face. "I had to kill a few people. I beat up some others. If the cops ever get me, I got enough information to plea bargain myself into a lighter sentence. You want to be me?" Then my father told me why he deserted me.

* * *

The Monday after the Sunday my father looked at his two boys and realized he had nothing to say to them, he and Johnny Dexter walk into Don Smiley's bar, which is mainly a shack where pot deals take place. This is their usual plan. My father is a compact, two-hundred pound ramrod, and carries a gat in his jeans pocket. Johnny has his shirttail out so that he covers the nine ml. stuck in the back of his pants. First they talk, then my father rams. By this time, they usually have some earnest money. If not, Johnny waves the 9 ml. They have yet to actually use it.

So inside Smiley's bar, Johnny Dexter and my father stand on the customer side of the bar with Don Smiley in between them on the other side. Don has a trimmed beard and round glasses, like a professor. He knows who they are. "Fellas look, this don't have to get ugly. I got the money. I really do. It's just tied up right now."

Don pulls two beers up and places them in front of Johnny and my father. "On the house," he says.

"Hell, I'd hope it's on the house," Johnny says, and my father drops his head, disappointed in Johnny's manner. My father is more business-like than Johnny or Don.

"Look, I've been knowing Snake Popp for fifteen years now. You just go back and tell him I'm good for it. He'll tell you."

"Who you think sent us?" Johnny asks.

"What's in the cash register?" my father asks.

"That's for my family. That's how I make my living," Smiley says.

My father reaches across the bar, knocking his beer bottle over, grabs Don by his shirt front, and yanks him over the bar. As Don clears the bar, my father jerks up, but Don's shirt rips, and Don falls to the ground on my father's side of the bar. Quickly, Johnny kicks Don in the head and the side. "Fuck you're good for it," Johnny says. "Snake wants you to pay now.'"

My father bends over and grabs shreds of Don's shirt and jerks him back up. "Now is there any need for us to do this?" my father asks in a sincere voice.

"I say we kick the shit out of him," Johnny says.

"You got to show some earnest money," my father says. "That's just the way it works."

"I'll show you earnest'," Don says. "Look behind you." Johnny jumps to one side, and my father slowly turns around to see Don's wife, Lula, holding a .38 pistol at her arm's length, pointed at his chest.

"You two get out of here," she says. While Lula keeps both arms straight and stiff with both hands wrapped around the butt and pokes the gun at my father's chest, Johnny slides one foot to the other to get around beside her. And when Don grabs a beer bottle and beans my father, spraying beer and glass across the bar, my father slides to the floor. Before my father hits the floor, Johnny has this .9 ml out, but before he can start shooting, Lula deliberately squeezes the trigger and sends a bullet into Johnny.

My father comes up with Lula in his arms. He clobbers her with one fist, then pulls the pistol away with his other hand. Lula is now on the ground and groaning like Johnny. Don advances toward Lula, and my father is not sure what Don intends. "You settle down," he says to Don, but Don with a shattered beer bottle in his hand keeps advancing. So my father shoots Don with Don's wife's revolver. Lula grabs his ankle, and my father feels a knife or razor blade cutting at the back of his calf, as though Lula is trying to sever in Achilles tendon. Not flinching, aiming carefully so as to not hit his own foot, my father shoots Lula.

My father squints through the blood and tastes it. It is running down his face from the crack on top of his head. Johnny has a strained look on his face that begs my father. My father knows his options. He can drag Johnny out, get him to Dee or Snake, and then hide out. That would work best if Lula and Don are dead, but he is not sure, and he does feel like putting more bullets into them. He can call for an ambulance and just leave town, but he is not yet that desperate. Or he could call the police and plead self-defense. He looks at Johnny, who shakes his head and pleads with his eyes.

My father goes to Johnny, grabs him, and drags him out the door. My father gets the shoulder of his pullover shirt bloody when he stands Johnny up, pushes a shoulder into him, and then leans him up against the passenger-side door of the car. He opens the door and stuffs groaning

Johnny into the car.

He limps back into the Smileys' bar. Neither husband nor wife move, and my father thinks that surely they are dead. He finds Johnny's gun and sticks it in his belt.

He finds the Smiley's gun and wipes all his prints off of it with a bar towel, for good measure, not sure why, he pours a beer over it. Then with the same bar towel, he tries to sop up his and Johnnie's blood. But mostly he just mixes the blood up, but that is okay too. Because that way, the ballistics experts—if Odessa has any—can't tell who killed who from what direction. The Smileys were both killed by their own gun, so he decides to leave it. He thinks some more, goes to the cash register, opens it pulls out the money. The police, he hopes, will think that it is small-time robbery or that the couple just started shooting each other.

He gets another bar towel, wraps it around his calf, and notices the blood seeping into his shoes and the sting in his leg. He looks in the bar mirror and sees his blood-wet hair and the trail of dried blood down his forehead. He limps back out to the truck. He drives to Johnny's apartment, pulls screaming Johnny out of the car, opens the door and pushes him into the apartment. "Bleed some," my father says. Johnny screams, my father grabs him, drags him back out to the truck, stuffs him in, and drives him to the hospital. My father stops the car and parks it just short of the Emergency Room. "Johnny, can you hear me?" Johnny screams. "You were fucking around with your gun, and it went off."

"But it ain't my gun shot me," Johnny screams.

"But I'm hoping the bullet in you is all fragmented so they ain't going to be sure whose gun it came from. And listen, now you listen Johnny Dexter, this is your truck. Hard as it was, much as it hurt, you drove yourself here. You got it? You ain't seen me." Then as much as it hurts, my father runs, and then he walks, and then he calls Snake.

By early afternoon, he sits in the Cactus Lounge with Snake and Dee. The stitches on his leg feel stiff; the ones on his head feel tight; he is light-headed from the pain pills; and he is afraid, as the nurse at the quick clinic told him, that he might have had a tendon damaged and needs to go to a hospital. But Snake did not drive him to a hospital but to the Cactus Lounge.

Snake Popp sits with his head in his hands and mutters, "Oh Christ, what we going to do? I can't think." He is so busy pushing his hands through his silver hair that he cannot take the cigarette out of his mouth and flick the ashes off.

"Nothing," Dee says. "You ought to be proud of Colton and Johnny. They did just as they should of. It's not going to be a clear case."

"So what is going to happen?" my father asks.

"They could shut me down," Snake says and rubs his head.

"They could piece together a bunch of things, and you could do some jail time. But its clearly self-defense. All you've done is fail to report what happened."

"What if Johnny talks?" my father asks.

"Oh shit," Snake says.

"Then you definitely do some time. But if he knows what's good for him, he won't say nothing."

"Oh, Jesus," Snake says.

Dee turns to him, her hard eyes focusing on him, "Snake, you ever figure you ought to get ought of the gambling business?"

"I'm gone," Snake says. As my father and Dee think that he means he's giving up his gambling nights, Snake rises and walks to the door.

"Snake," Dee shouts after him. "You can play this one of several ways. We discussed the best way. We keep our stories straight."

"I got it," Snake grumbles.

They watch him go, and Dee turns her hard eyes to my father. "I been through this before. It's best if you just clear out and forget who you are for awhile."

"I can't just leave," my father says.

"I got a friend in Dallas could use a guy like you."

"I thought I could work for you?"

"You did real good today from your story. My friend could use a guy skilled in those areas."

My father can't think, so he drinks most of his bottle of beer. As long as he is in this blur, he figures he might as well plunge in. "I got a family," my father says.

"My friend pays very well for the skills he needs. He needs a man can come out on the winning side of barroom gunfight."

My father reaches toward his ankle and feels the bandage, feels the slight moisture where the blood is soaking through, considers taking another Darvon. "But my family needs more from me than money."

Dee chuckled, "And just what is that? And what is it you figure you're giving them?"

My father tries to get his mind to see through the fog in his head, tries to get his mouth to make the right words, but nothing comes to him.

"You probably heard me say that, if you look at a whore real close, you can see she ain't got no soul. That's only part of the story. They aren't born without souls. Somewhere along the way they lose them. I know. I used to run whores. I used to be a whore."

"I'm not a whore," my father says.

Dee doesn't even laugh. "I had people help me. I tried to repay them. So now, I'm helping you."

"I got two boys," my father says.

"So now make money. The sad fact is all you got left to give your family is money."

"God damn it, shut up," my father says.

"God damn it, listen," Dee says.

"I got a choice."

"Ain't no choice in something like this. You're beyond choice. You just got to have the smarts and the balls to recognize the obvious."

Still later, after a few hours of sleep in Dee's office, my father stumbles through his small house on Adams Street. He makes his way into the living room where he hears voices. Raul is in front of the TV in a recliner sleeping. His snoring mixes with the chatter from the late night TV show.

My father makes his way down the hall to my mother's room, slowly opens their door so as not to wake her, looks at her sleeping, and looks at the side of the bed that should be his. For a long time, all that he and my mother have done in that bed is sleep.

He backs out of the bedroom and goes to one farther down the hall. He opens the door to look in. I am sleeping there in my bunk bed with my brother above me. We cannot know that our father is studying our faces because he will not know us beyond this night.

By early morning, before daybreak, my father watches spaced drops of rain splatter on his windshield. He sees *Fort Worth 45 miles* on a green and white sign in front of him. By the time people are heading off to work, he will be in Dallas with a name, a phone number, and an address that Dee gave him. He wishes he could be a better father.

* * *

With my father's money, I made some choices. I figured that part of my problem was Odessa, so I moved to San Angelo, got admitted probationally to Angelo State University, and got out with a degree in P.E. I found a wife and a job coaching middle school football and teaching history in Denver City, Texas. Denver City is dry, so I have to buy my beer in a New Mexico County, and when I drink my beer, I have to hide the bottles in an old bag and put then in the trash, so that the Church of Christ superintendent doesn't know how much I drink. My wife and I have two girls. I take them all for shopping trips to Lubbock, to camping trips in Carlsbad, for long weekends in a Holiday Inn in Dallas or Fort Worth. So I think that I know my wife and girls better than my father knew his wife and boys. Sometimes, when we are in Denver City, we sit out in the backyard, each of us with a drink, look at the rolling land beyond our backyard, and wait or wish for something to happen.

I have just buried my father. I have no idea how Dee Price even knew what had become of me, but she called me and said that his casket was delivered by freight and dropped off at the bus company. My signature was the one they needed. I stood in the living room of my modest 1700 square foot house in Denver City with my wife busy exercising out on the back porch and my girls playing in the air-conditioning inside. I walked past my girls who did not look up from their dolls and coloring books and looked out the French doors at my wife practicing her yoga. I just figured that there just ought to be more of something even though I didn't know more of what.

My father had prepared well for his death. Along with the casket was a registered check for expenses, a funeral plot, and handwritten will. My father spread his money out to everyone: me, my mother, Dee Price, Snake Popp, Raul, and my brother doing his second hitch in prison. Everyone was equal, except I got to be the manager, the coach, the quarterback for his death.

As per his request, we had no service, but gathered to watch as they lowered him into the ground. My mother didn't shed a tear. Raul, my grandfather, just shook his head. My mother hugged me, and Raul shook my hand. They had raised me, but somewhere along the way, after my father appeared again and talked to me, we lost each other, same with my brother. He went to prison and couldn't stay out; I went to Denver City and my own family.

After the funeral, after refusing the offer to stay with my mother, I walked to my pickup truck and found Dee leaning against the door. "Why don't you come by the Cactus Lounge?"

"I got to get back home."

"You got to know how your father died. His will ain't completely executed yet."

So I walked through the sunbeams and dust at the Cactus Lounge, now under its fifth or sixth owner, but still housing Dee Price's office.

She sat at a table in front of the office door with a beer already waiting for me. She rose when I walked up and smiled. Her smile seemed to make her face crack. The forked scar across her forehead and cheek now competed with the other cracks in her face. The West Texas heat and dryness cooked and baked most people, so we were all headed for looking leathery, especially a coach who squinted into the sun during the two hottest months of the year. Dee seemed to have gotten some extra baking. She was thin to begin with, but now she was extra skinny. Her eyes had a slightly yellowish tint. Though she tried not to be, she was scary. "Sit," she said. I sat behind a beer.

The door to her office opened, and Snake Popp stepped out. He stuck out his hand, and I shook it. Snake was about Dee's age. He was tanned but not wrinkled. He wore a starched Guyabara shirt and just as crisply starched cotton slacks and beige loafers with no socks on. He had a tiny silver earring that matched his silver hair. He sipped from a Bloody Mary in a clear glass.

Dee started, "Your father was an assassin, a hit man. He got hit."

Snake took over, "The casket was closed because he was a mess."

"But he gave it hell right to the very end," Dee said. "I suppose you kind of know why he left Odessa."

"Last I saw him, he gave me some clues.'

"Johnny Dexter, his partner, wasn't so lucky. He had to get out of the business because that bullet lodged in his spine. So he ended up in a wheel chair." Dee grunted, "Course he is still alive." She looked at Snake. "He works for Snake."

"And does pretty good for himself, thank you kindly," Snake said.

"So you doing good?" Snake asked.

"Okay," I said. "I'm a coach."

"We know," Snake said. They both shifted in their chairs.

"Look, we figure we owe your father," Dee said. "So we wanted to help you."

"How much is that coaching job paying you?" Snake asked.

"Not enough," I said. By this time the boom had kind of come back. It wasn't as wild as the last one, but wildcatters were drilling, and Odessa was busy. I had talked with my wife about deserting Denver City and coming back to the money that was flowing through Odessa. With the sunbeams and dust drifting in from the cracks, the Cactus Lounge turned sort of golden.

"I'm mostly retired now, but Dee might be able to use somebody."

"I got people like your dad and what Johnny Dexter used to be working for me. They do what you did. But I need someone with some smarts. Someone to kind of take over some of the day-to-day affairs."

I shifted in my seat. Snake shifted in his seat, ran his hands up the side of his head to give his head a pair of sliver wings. "I'll leave you to it," he said to Dee. "I'm more settled now."

His shoes squished as he crossed the wooden floor, and he let in a flood of sunlight when he opened the door. When he closed it, my eyes adjusted on Dee. "So is this a real job you're offering me?"

"Yes."

"Would I need a gun like when I was repoing cars and emptying vending machines?"

"Not unless you want one." I stared over her shoulder and felt like I was back in Denver City in my backyard wishing. Dee started talking again. "If you look at a whore real close, you can see she ain't got no soul. That's only part of the story. They aren't born without souls. Somewhere along the way they lose them."

"I know."

Dee seemed to stare over my shoulder, but I looked at her eyes. "The point is, you can lose your soul doing most anything."

"Like working for you." I was sorry for being mean.

"Or being a coach in Denver City." Dee nodded her head to herself. "Look, you may not believe it, but I'm trying to do something good here."

"What about my father? Did he lose his soul?" Dee said nothing. "What about you?" I asked.

"I said you could tell with whores. I ain't a whore no more."

"Was my father?"

Dee looked around and saw no one. She pushed herself up, went behind the bar, and came back with two bottles of beer. "Let me tell you about your father." So she did through several more beers. But mostly the story was about her life and crimes and regrets.

That night, my wife and two girls and I went out to the backyard and waited for the sun to set. As are most sunsets in West Texas, it was beautiful, but it wasn't enough. I felt the itch that my father must have felt when he lived in Odessa. I felt very alone with my wife and daughters. But when the sun finally, fully set and I sat looking at the dark with the women in my life, I decided to keep wanting and wishing with them.

Bankers

I got a fair amount of money and a certain degree of respect among my business associates. I consider myself a salesman. I provide things for people. Which is different from a banker. But long time ago, I could have become a banker.

Here is how it was. I am just graduated high school and have no clue about what I'm going to do with my life. College seems like some foreign country, so I take the tests but only apply at San Antonio Junior College. My mother and several friends told me to go to college and study enough to make Ds so as to stay out of the war with a college deferment. My father said he fought for his country and so his son should fight for his country so's I should just wait to be drafted. I didn't know if he meant it was just his country or I had a part of it too.

Most of my friends from the Southside had working people like my parents, so they just didn't know what to do. Of course, I had schoolmates who enlisted, who went off to some college land, or who smoked a lot of pot and became hippies. So I figured just to go back to work for the downtown bank I had worked at the summer before and wait to decide or see what happened.

My father said I should be careful of that bank. He showed me the headlines. Steves Bank, started by one of San Antonio's old, rich German families, got bought out by Sammy White, this south Texas rancher and businessman who was being sued by half the state. Sammy White had a habit, my father said, of turning things to shit while he came out smelling like a rose.

But I went back to work for the Steves Bank anyway. At first, because I liked downtown, especially in the summer mornings when the stores would send their cleaning crews to hose off the sidewalks, outside tables and chairs. They'd wash away the spilled beer, piss, puke, or whatever was on those sidewalks and get ready for another pounding from a hot afternoon. Downtown mornings, for me, was the smell of hose water on warming concrete and little rainbow arches filtering through the spray. It was all fresh and new and clean in the morning, making me think my life would just work out. So I'd catch the second earliest express bus to downtown and walk around right up until bank opening time. I'd even walk through alleys, through the sterno cans, wine bottles, and pigeon bones, waking up the bums, and thinking, who knows, but what I might end up eating pigeons in a downtown alley. Typical of me back then, I'd figure that being a bum might even have its plus side.

So in I walk for my first day, back to my little cubbyhole where I help the head teller, and there to greet me is Emmitt. Emmitt is this old guy nearly eighty who retired as a bank vice president years before and then when his wife died, went back to work at a bank. Banking is just what he does. He dresses banking style. He wears a coat and tie, but when he takes off his coat he has these old sleeve garters pushed up to his elbows. And when he is stooped over counting for a long time, he wears one of those tinted eye shades. Emmett's eyes are sunk deep in his head with dark circles all around them. He's got hair growing out his ears and nose, and his eyebrows are twisted into points like the old-time moustaches, but his head is slick, shiny bald with some rough, brown splotches on it. When he sees me, his old eyes get watery, and this old man hugs me.

Then I notice on the top of his slick old head is the shape of a perfect pair of red lips. I wipe at it with my fingers. "What's this?" I ask.

Then Becky, prettiest of the tellers, looks over and says, "I got to kiss my boyfriends."

Doris, the head teller, gives me my orders, which are the same every day. While dumpy Doris, with her curled-toe, elf slippers, sucks on her cigarettes and peers out the window of her office to watch the younger, prettier tellers some of who tease me about being young and manly and able, I grab the bagged coins collected the day before and dump them into the coin rolling machine and watch it as it sputters and tries to spit out rolls of quarters, nickels, dimes, or pennies. Sometimes it just chokes, and the coins and the paper rolls gush out of the chute. So then I sweep and scoop up all the spilled coins and dump them back in the machine while Doris frowns at me and the machine.

After spilling coins in the morning, I'd work with Emmitt in the afternoons, and he'd train me to be a teller. The year before, with his garter sleeves and visor on, he taught me how to grab a stack of bills, bend back a corner, and flip through them by fives with my thumb. He could count money faster than anybody in the bank, faster than the machine that could only count crisp, new bills, and after he closed out at the end of the day, he'd help out all the pretty teller girls. When I first worked with him, we had run out of calculator paper and I was changing it, and he yelled, "Don't throw away that roll." I held up the empty cardboard paper roll, and he nodded and said "When the circus comes to town, they buy those to make assholes for hobby horses." He'd smile when he said a joke like that; then he'd just go back to counting money. And the tellers would giggle and sometimes kiss him on the forehead.

And the summer before was Hemisfair year, so all sorts of freaks and crooks would come in. So these two short-change artists come in. They were dressed flashy in colors so bright you had to squint at them. So while one guy was scooting around the bank, the other guy comes up to Emmitt and asks for change for a hundred in twenties and tens and fives. Emmitt motions me over, and I watch as the guy then asks for change for a twenty, then for a fifty, and Emmitt interrupts him and asks if he didn't want a different bill. Turns out Emmitt gyped the short-change guy and kept him there long enough for a downtown beat cop to escort him out. Then there was the time Emmitt calls me over and tells me to stare long and hard at two twenties he was counting. When I held them up the light, I could see short thin red and blue veins, but they looked drawn. And so they were. So Emmitt lets me call the F.B.I. and give them the report, and the F.B.I. and some guys from the Secret Service and the Federal Reserve come look at the bills and thank me for my sharp eyes.

So on my first day back, after rolling coins, I'm at lunch, eating a sandwich in our little lunch room and looking at the sizzling concrete outside, and Emmitt comes up to me. He has his carrots and celery all cut in nice pieces just about all the same length, and he has his tuna fish on white bread with the crust cut off. He was classy like that. "So, Gregory," always "Gregory," he says, not "Greg," "are you considering your future?" Whenever somebody older said future, I always figured I was getting a lecture.

"I'm mostly waiting on my future to find me," I say.

Emmitt smiles, "You know, anymore, a banker needs a degree."

"So you think I could be a banker?"

"I'm not just talking about being a teller, now Gregory, but I'm talking about being a loan officer, a Vice President even."

"So you think that I could do that."

"I don't know. You have to study. You have keep up with the banking world."

"I could do that."

"Yes, I think you can. But you should want to. People forget that bankers help people. Bankers make things possible for people." He waits to see if I'm thinking or not. "You ought to go to college, then become a banker."

I start nodding my head and munching from my sandwich while Emmitt takes a dainty bite out of his tuna fish, "But now," Emmitt leans closer and lowers his voice. "Be careful of this bank."

I lean across the lunch room table and my forehead nearly touches Emmitt's. "What's wrong with this bank?"

"The new owner. He doesn't appreciate banking."

Emmitt leans away from me and frowns while he chews his sandwich. From the lines in his forehead and the way his eyes seemed to sink back further into his forehead, I can see that Sammy White scares poor ol' Emmitt.

So, I close out the day with Emmitt. Emmitt and me go into the main vault, and we look at the bagged money and we count it. With Emmitt looking over my shoulder and smiling because I got faster from the last summer, I count the bags of old bills that we have stashed and will soon be sending over to the Federal Reserve building to be burned.

Since then, I've thought a lot about the life of that money and the use it served and the way it must have helped people and maybe even hurt them and then of it all just going up in smoke and out the chimney above the Reserve. And back then, with that money in front of me is when I actually started thinking I would like to be a banker.

And Emmitt must have been thinking too because, when I turn around from counting the money in record time, and this my first day, he is smiling at me. "Well, my, my, you just tugged right on through that little chore," Emmitt says to me. Emmitt nods serious-like, but then a little light flickered inside Emmitt's scarred, bald head, and he starts smiling again,

"Gregory, do you play tennis?"

"I've tried."

"Would you like to try this Saturday?" Emmitt asks me, and I say "Sure."

And after work, with the heat bouncing off the sidewalks and boiling me, I walk a little around downtown, by the old public library with its cement lion and elephant out front and sit on the steps in the shade. I get just a little cooler. Over to my left, down the street, next to the river is the site of the new glass library building. And soon, they will move all the books out of this building, and the cement lion and elephant won't have the people gawking at them and the kids pretending to ride them. And to my right in the distance, looking over the simmering city is the Tower of America, built for Hemisfair. And two years before, it was just a pole sticking into the sky. And I start to think about my future. The war comes sneaking back up on me as well as the idea of college.

And for a while there, that day, I thought that Emmitt's idea about what a banker was was what I should be.

* * *

So, that Saturday, at noon, I drive the clunker that my father bought for me, a '61 Plymouth Valiant with a pushbutton transmission under the dash, to San Pedro Park tennis courts. Emmitt is there waiting for me in his tennis outfit. He has shorts down to about his knees, and his legs bow out from those white shorts. He has on a white tennis shirt with an orange stripe on the collar and down the short sleeves. He's got a bucket-like tennis hat squshed on his head. He has a racket under one arm, another racket in his hand, and a cooler in his other hand. "You want to warm up?" Emmitt says to me.

So I jog to the far side of a court, and I peek over my shoulder at Emmitt hobbling up behind me, old-man style. It's like he needs both those bowed legs under him at the same time, so he won't tip over. So I figure that I can beat the hell out of this guy taking those choppy steps. I get to the far side of the court, watch, and jump in place, noticing that sweat has already started to run down my forehead into my eyes and that the sun seems to be pressing on the top of my head. Emmitt sets the cooler down near the tall fence and then quick steps to the court. He still has both rackets one in his hand and one under his arm. He bends over, then makes his body just sort of shake, like a wet dog. Then he pulls a tennis ball out of his pocket, bounces it, and hits it to me.

I watch the ball and try to give it a hard whack back over the net. And then I notice, Emmitt is playing with a racket in each hand. He lobs the ball into one corner of the court, and I have to run to get to it. I whack it hard again, just over the net. Emmitt shuffles to the ball and just gets a racket under it to lob it again to the far corner of court. And I run to get it. The old fart is ambidextrous. He runs slower than a girl, but I can get nothing past him because he's got nearly six feet of range with those two rackets. And all he does is lob, and I run. I beat him for the point. Then I beat him the first game. But my knees feel weak. And my eyes are blurred and burning with sweat in them. So I ask for a drink. I get a drink, Emmitt doesn't.

So this old man baby-stepping up and back, right and left around the court, lobbing nearly every shot, me taking long tugs at the water after every game, just wears my ass out. He beats me 6-3, for set, and asks if I want to play another one. I am so tired I can't even talk, but Emmitt glances up at the sun and says, "We better not push it. Sunstroke weather." I smile and try to jog to him, but I can barely make my feet work. After I take a drink, he upends the water over his head and smiles at me while he drips. And when he leaves, he climbs into his twelve-year-old Rambler and waves real rapid-like to me as he pulls out of the tennis courts' parking lot.

I had to think about Emmitt that whole weekend. I mean, I thought he was attached to the bank. I couldn't imagine him outside of the little teller's booth he was in. And here he is kicking kids' assess in tennis and, from remembering his little grin, I couldn't help but think he was kinda proud of the ass kicking.

* * *

By the time I get back to work on Monday, I'm actually thinking better and better of Emmitt. When I dare to, I turn my back to the coin rolling machine and go out and stare at him and catch him napping a time or two. And I'm thinking even harder about college and some degree and then a life as a banker counting old money, catching short-change artists, finding counterfeit money, helping people when I hear a scream, and then Doris yelling at me to run downstairs.

I zap out the Head Teller's office and then out the door of the filing room, into the upstairs lobby, and then I run down the down escalator, three steps at a time, until I'm in front of the automatic door next to the street, and I'm looking at this whimpering, pregnant Mexican girl, sprawled out on the floor inside the bank. And to one side of her is square-faced, Brylcreemed Hank Worley, one of Steves' vice presidents, and to the other side of her is a man in a LBJ hat, string tie, blue-striped seersucker suit, pointy-toed boots, and a wet umbrella. I think to look up and see there is a sheet of rain outside, and I see what has happened. Somebody forgot to put the rubber mat inside the door, and this poor girl steps in from out of the rain, slips on the hard, slick tiles, and cracks her ass on the floor. The LBJ cowboy and Hank exchange looks, and then the woman screams: "Sue."

Not really thinking, I step forward, slip a little myself, and try to help the lady up. When I grab her arm and she tries to let me pull her up, she blurts out in pain as she tries to put her foot down. "Shit," I hear Hank say.

I kind of half drag and half carry her to the carpet and let her lie down, and I hear, "Who is this boy?"

"This is Gregory Newman," Hank Worley says. "He works here summers."

The girl snivels and says, "Sue."

"Well, he seems to know how to handle hisself," the LBJ cowboy says. And I see some keys dangling in front of me. "Mr. Gregory, can you drive?"

"Yes sir," I say.

"Those keys are to my wife's Cadillac. It's parked in the garage in my space. You pull it out front. Treat her real nice, but get her into the back seat all comfortable, and then get her to the emergency room at Santa Rosa. And then you stay with her and make sure she's happy."

"What's your space?" I ask. Hank Worley breathes in.

"It's the big one, right next to the door," the man says.

"This is Mr. White," Hank says.

Mr. White says, "I'm the fella owns about sixty-percent of this place."

"Sue," the woman says.

"Will do," I say, grab the keys, and turn around. Up at the second floor, looking down at me and nodding his head, like he just woke up from his nap, is ol' Emmitt.

I run out the backdoor of the bank, take a right, and duck into the underground parking lot, and sure enough, sitting in its place with a sign saying Mr. White is Sammy White's wife's lime green Cadillac with a white vinyl top. I open the door and slide in on the white leather seat. Before I start it up, I just rub on that seat to get the slick, oiled feel of the leather. Then I start it up, and I turn on the air. I find the knob for the radio and click in on and turn the dial to hear and feel the throb from the back speakers.

By the time I get to the front of the bank and barely remember to turn off the radio, Hank and Mr. Sammy White have the crying lady by the arms and are guiding her toward the curb. People stop and stare. Hank opens the backseat passenger door as smiling Sammy White guides her in, then gently pushes her across the backseat so that she is laying across it. I shiver when she muffles a scream, and I look at Hank's face in the open passenger side door, and his face tells me I better not fuck up.

As I'm trying to remember which downtown streets go which way and around what to get to Santa Rosa, the lady in back sniffles. I glance in the rearview mirror and see tears on her face. With my left hand on the wheel, I reach behind the front seat with my right, and she grabs my hand and squeezes it. And then she says, again, "Sue."

So I eventually pull into the emergency room, open the backdoor, and help the limping lady into the hospital. It is mid morning, but already, bleeding and otherwise hurt people are crowding in. I reach for her purse, and first she tugs it away from me, but then lets me have it. I find a wallet and a fake looking social security card and a driver's license. She screams. Then I start screaming. And soon, I have nurses around me, and I'm trying to explain that the woman is hurt, and they explain that the woman has no insurance, and I yell louder. They say that they need to contact the next of kin. Then I yell that I am the next of kin. When they look at me, something takes possession of me, and I say, "That's right. What you looking at? I'm her husband."

"What's your wife's name?"

"Maria Newman."

"How you going to pay for this visit?"

"Do we look like we can pay for this?"

So I suddenly have a lot of forms in front of me, and I am writing down Maria Newman and wishing I could have thought faster and come up with some other name. And then they get that pregnant lady into a wheelchair, and I hold her hand, and she cries, and she motions I should bend over her so she can tell me something. And with her hot breath on my ear, she says a number. "Su Esposo?" I ask. She nods, and then, I phone her husband.

Emilio isn't too good with English either, but he is better than her. And he makes me to understand that he will be at the hospital as soon as he can. So then I call Hank Worley, and he says to stay there until I am sure how she is. And then he says, "You see if this sue' idea stays in her head."

"What about Mr. White's car?"

"I've already talked to him about that. You drive the car back to the bank when you get through." But Hank Worley keeps breathing into the phone, like he isn't through talking to me yet. "Now you be careful with that car," he says.

So I wait and wait. I'm drinking cokes and eating chips and peanut butter crackers from the vending machine. Finally, they wheel that lady back and tell me her husband that she has a sprained ankle and knee and that our baby is fine. A nurse says she is more scared than anything, so they pumped her up with some sedatives. She smiles at me and, she reaches up from her wheelchair and takes my hand again. The nurse tells me that my wife is dismissed.

I wheel her out of the hospital, and then I have to give the wheelchair back, so she stands up and puts the new crutches under her arm. We walk to a bench under a cottonwood, sit in the still damp air, and wait for Emilio. Her name is Tristina. And she tells me she will not sue. And when Emilio shows up, she hugs him, and he picks her up off the ground, and I follow behind them carrying her crutches as Emilio carries her to his pickup and stuffs her in the cab, and I throw the crutches in the back. The last I see of that pretty, scared lady, she has her head swiveled around to look out the back windshield of the truck to see me waving goodbye.

Now, still, I think about that woman once in awhile. Mostly, she wasn't hurt, but she was scared. English was new to her, probably the city was new too, and she was just about to panic. And I can look back and figure that this was where Emmitt's notion of banking comes in. I was helping her. I was kind of a banker. But when I think that, I remember that the word the coming out her mouth was "sue." Everybody is always selling something.

So, by the time I get back to the bank, it is closed. I pull Sammy White's Cadillac up to the backside of the building right next to the parking garage. And there, sitting on the bench the tellers put out so they could have lunch outside on nice days is Mr. Sammy White, pretty as you please, eating an orange. He has his seersucker suit coat folded up and sitting behind him, and he has his LBJ hat pulled low over his eyes. I get out the Cadillac and inch toward Mr. White. "Have a sit," he says.

I sit beside Mr. White. He looks out at the steam from rain rising off the asphalt and cement and cuts a slice out of his orange with his pocket knife. He spears that slice of orange with his pocket knife blade and pokes it toward me. "Orange slice?" he asks. I thank him and take the slice of orange. "You know, one of the reasons I bought this bank is I like the smell of water from a hose splashing on cement, they kind of way it splashes up and makes everything feel cleaner."

"I know just exactly what you mean," I say. He pokes another slice at me. I pull it from the knife, bite into it, and feel the spray of orange juice inside my mouth.

"But this evaporating rain makes it all steamy. It's nasty."

"I would have got you your car back, but Mr. Worley told me to wait, and they just couldn't get that woman fixed."

"So did she say anymore about suing?"

"She's not going to sue."

"How do you know?"

"She was just scared."

"You sure?"

"She told me she wasn't."

"You believe her?"

96

"Yes."

Sammy White slides another slice of orange to me and pops the last slice into his mouth. "Then I'd say you done a fair day's work."

"Sorry, I didn't get your car back."

"You like that car?"

"That's a nice car, sir."

"Good job, Gregory." He stands up, walks to the car, and looks over it. "Toss me the keys." I toss him the keys. He opens up the door, throws his suit coat in, then he throws his LBJ hat in and turns to me. "I'll see you at work, Gregory. I might have another job for you."

* **

So the next day, Doris slips into her curly-toed elf shoes, sucks on her cigarette, and shakes her head as she listens to me. Emmitt, who gets his run of the whole teller area in back of the counter, even Doris's office, listens and rubs his flat palm over his shiny but patchy bald head. "That should never have happened," Doris says.

"Looks like you might have saved the bank some money," Emmitt says. "You did well."

I puff out for Emmitt, but then he adds, "But now you be careful of that Sammy White."

"He seems like an alright guy to me," I say.

"You be careful," he says, and I go back to rolling my coins.

But then midweek comes, and with Doris gawking, I get a call on Doris' phone. Now let me repeat that, I get a call. I am nobody and somebody is calling on Doris' phone. And Doris' face scrunches all up and then just drops, showing wrinkles I had never seen before. And she slowly lowers the phone from her ear and says, "Mr. White wants to see you."

I can feel Emmitt's eyes staring at my back as I round Doris' office door. And waiting by the executive office is square-faced, slick-haired Hank Worley telling me just with his eyes not to fuck up. And then Hank Worley opens the door for me.

In I step. And there behind his mahogany desk, under one of those bluebonnet and wagon wheel pictures, is Sammy White cracking pecans with his hands. He puts two nuts together, then squeezes them between

97

his clasped palms, and I hear a crack. Then he pulls the cracked nut apart and digs at the meat with his pocket knife. "People do good for me, I like to do good by them."

"Thank you sir," I say and notice that there's this chair in front of him, but he doesn't ask me to sit, just stares at those pecans.

"You like that Cadillac?"

"Oh yes, sir."

"How'd you like to go on a little road trip?"

"Fine sir."

"How you like to take a brand new, just bought Cadillac on that road trip?"

"Sir?"

"Reason I had my wife's Cadillac was I was shopping for her a new one. And I found one. So I want you to drive that new Cadillac down to my ranch the other side of Freer, pick up my Cadillac, and drive it back."

He looks intently at his pecan, opens his palms to look at his reward, gouges out some pecan meat, chews, and then smiles at me. "And here's some pecans for you." And Sammy White, the man himself, gets up from his desk and rounds its corner and hands me a sack of pecans and the keys to his wife's new Cadillac. "You can eat them nuts on the way down. Best get started. It's a drive to get there in back in one day."

* **

Mrs. Sammy White's new Cadillac is a kind of a maroon with another white leather interior. The radio is top quality and nearly shatters the windows. And in the glove compartment is Mrs. White's 8-track collection, mostly country western and some soft, syrupy stuff by Andy Williams. But I make my way through most all of her tapes as I cruise through the cactus fields and staring cattle, eating my boss's pecans then on to Freer and past and then down a paved country road to a double-wide gate over a cattle guard with White Ranch written on an arch stretching over the gate. Then I drive another mile on, get this on a paved road, up to the long, low, new ranch house.

I pull up in front, walk up the curving stone sidewalk, and knock on the door. A woman with several strands of hair hanging in her face and some smeared mascara answers the door. Then I see more. She has on a bikini top with cleavage trying to push that top off, a pair of Wrangler jeans, and boots. In her hand is one of those fancy drink glasses with the long stem up under a bowl, and what I guess is a margarita or martini is splashing out the sides of that glass. "Mrs. White?" I ask.

The woman steps past me to look out across the front yard to the Cadillac parked at the end of the sidewalk. "That's mine, I'm guessing," she says and sways in front of me. And I'm noticing for an older woman she has her butt packed into her Wranglers as nice as she has her chest packed into that bikini top.

"Brand new Cadillac," I say. And she turns around and walks right past me, and without turning around says, "Name is Cheryl. You want a drink."

"No, I don't think I want a drink. In fact, I better get back because it's a long drive, and I don't have much daylight, and I'm on the clock so to speak..."

"Come in," Cheryl White says, and I know that it is an order, and she is my boss's wife, so I follow her in, and she shuts the door after me. I keep walking, figuring I'm in a living room, but it's so damn big I walk and walk and can't figure out where I'm going. I pass a sofa and come up to another one, and then I get my order, "Stop."

Mrs. White pours me whatever she is having into a glass like hers, and carrying my glass and hers in one hand and the pitcher in the other, sloshing liquor out of the glasses and the pitcher, she steps toward me all slinky-like and hands me the glass "Sit," she orders. I sit on the sofa. "Can I take that pitcher from you?" I ask. She hands it to me with one hand, and I take it and realize that this woman must have some hell of some muscles from hauling that pitcher of liquor around the house with her, and I sit it on a lamp table with both hands. She hands me my drink, and I sip it. It is gin, nearly straight, and I start to cough.

"So what do you think is going on here?" Mrs. White asks me.

I take another sip of the gin, which to me tastes like carrot juice, and I say "I mean, well I don't know, you mean with me and you having a drink?"

"I mean with fucking everything." She takes her wet napkin from her drink and wipes at her chest just above her cleavage. I take another sip of the carrot juice

"You're the wife of the boss."

"Right. So why do you think you drove my yearly gift down to me?"

"Mr. White's busy." I sip.

"Right. I get one new Cadillac a year. I thought I was worth more than that."

"I'm sure that Mr. White sees a lot of worth in you."

She sips from her drink and stares ahead, like she has forgotten I'm there. Then she starts talking without looking at me. "And I'm thinking maybe you are even a part of that gift." And then she looks at me as though she is disgusted. "Look what I traded my life for." She puts her drink down and reaches for a pack of cigarettes. She fumbles with it to get a cigarette out, and then she hands me a match and tells me, "Light my cigarette."

I do as I'm told and say, "Maybe, I ought to go."

Cheryl takes a puff and blows smoke ahead of her, and then she turns and blows smoke toward me. "Why do you think he's not here?"

"Who?"

"My husband, you dipshit," Cheryl says and stands up.

"I don't know."

With a cigarette in one hand and a drink spilling out of her other, she tells me. "Because it's boring as shit. So he's in San Antonio, in his apartment, playing like some cowboy come to town to buy most of it. And here I sit." She sucks on her cigarette. "Don't you wonder why he didn't give me my fan-fucking-tastic present? Why he isn't here, in person?"

"I'm young, Mam. I try not to think about those things."

"Well, it's not just what you're not thinking. It's that it's just so boring. He's got that bank. He's got his business interests. He's got Lord knows what else. And I got this."

"This don't look so bad," I say.

"I know. That's why I don't dare leave him. What else I got?" She looks at me like she's about to pounce on me, but I don't know if she'd pounce on me to tear off my clothes or beat the shit out of me. "Are you payment too? Is that what Sammy's thinking?"

Now I'm getting more than a little pissed. "I better be getting Mr. White's Cadillac."

"Sit down."

"I may be just a delivery boy, and I sure as hell am confused, but I can't help but thinking that me sitting down ain't going to do me or you no good."

She smiles. "You may regret not staying."

"I figure I'm going to have regrets no matter what I do now. So I'm just going to do what Mr. White told me to do."

She walks into the kitchen and comes with the straps of her purse slung over her forearm, she reaches into it and pulls out some keys. She flips them to me. "It's in the garage."

"Where's that?"

"Out the backdoor," and as I inch backward toward it, I try to memorize her standing there, puffing out smoke, swaying on her boot heels, sipping that drink, and looking like the very picture of my future regrets.

* * *

And so, just as I turn Mr. White's yellow Cadillac with the black vinyl top and the dark tinted windows out of the big gate and am kicking up dust because I got the heavy-foot, I see a pickup truck hauling ass behind me. I press the gas pedal harder, the truck closes in. As I'm looking in my rearview mirror, trying to see through the dust I'm kicking up, another pickup just suddenly appears in front of me. I see no roads, so the truck must have come cross country. I hit the horn. Then I hit the brakes to keep from running right up that pickup's ass. Then the other one pulls up right beside me. Dust is swirling all around us. I get out of the car, and yell, "Just what do you hillbillies, think you're doing?"

As the dust clears away, one man then another step out of the pickup trucks. The driver of the pickup now on the side of me has on a black suit, sunglasses, and slicked-back black hair. The other driver has on jeans, pointy-toed boots, a white shirt, and a straw cowboy hat. They look at me, then at each other, then in unison they duck into the cabs of their pickups. "Hey, who are you guys," I yell. One then the other comes out from the cabs of the pickups, and each one has a sawed-off shotgun. "You guys aren't cops are you?" I ask.

"Who are you?" the guy in the suit asks and points the sawed-off shotgun at me.

"Quein es?" the guy in the cowboy hat asks.

"I work for Mr. White."

"Where's he?" the black-suited man asks.

"At work. Where should he be?"

"You're a smart ass."

"Gringo child, why you have this car?" the man in the hat asks.

Then the sawed-off shotgun in the black-suited man's hands goes off, and I feel my shoulders jump up to my ears, and I jerk around to see a spray of holes ruining the yellow driver's door of Mr. White's Cadillac. The man in the cowboy hat fires his and takes out the grillwork. They both pump their shotguns, shoot again, and the tires become shreds of rubber.

"What the hell do you two cretins think Mr. White is going to say?"

The man in the suit walks up to me, and I can see the beads of sweat on his forehead, and he puts his arm around my shoulder, and I can smell him growing a little rank in that black suit. "You tell Mr. White' what you seen. And you tell him it's a little greeting from Fred Carrasco. Mr. Carrasco don't talk shit and don't play games."

"How am I supposed to tell him when you just killed my ride?" And then I think that I may have just gotten myself killed.

With his arm around me, the black-suited man leads me to his pickup and opens the passenger side door. "Get in," he says.

"What's your name?" I ask.

"You don't need to know my name," he says. "Get in." And the other guy starts walking toward me. I can run. I can beg. I can try to fight two sawed-off shotguns. Instead, I get in.

The black-suited man comes around to the driver's seat and puts the sawed-off shotgun across the rifle rack. "Don't touch that," he says.

The first pickup pulls away, and we follow leisurely behind. "Mrs. White is sure going to be pissed."

"You seen her?" the man asks.

"Who? Was there a woman at the wreck?"

"Mrs. White, dip shit."

"Yeah. I brought her the new Cadillac Mr. White bought her and was bringing his back to him."

"I hear she's hot."

"She's all right."

"I mean, I hear she's so pissed off at him, she'll do anybody just to get back at him."

"I couldn't say."

"Could you guess?"

"I wouldn't want to."

"You got a mouth and an attitude." I waited for a bullet, but the man smiled. "You should be careful who you work for."

"So who do you work for?"

"You heard."

"Fred Carrasco is a gangster. What's he got to do with Mr. White?"

"You better shut up now."

"Well, what's your name?"

"You better shut up now." The man in the black suit turns to me and pulls down his sunglasses to stare at me over the tops of his glasses to be sure I got the point.

I shut up, for awhile. "So what if it wouldn't have been me?"

"Shut up."

"But, I mean, what if it had been Mr. Sammy White in that car?"

"Shut the fuck up, you little shit ass." And I figure I had better shut up.

We drive to a gas station, and the man in the black suit nods to the attendant. He lowers his sunglasses, looks me up and down, and all but smiles. "You got a dime for a phone call?'

"You didn't rob me."

"You got balls, dip shit. Be careful you don't lose them," he says. "Get out."

With my dime, I call the bank and get Hank Worley and the tone in his voice tells me I fucked up big time.

* * *

I sit on the coke machine the long flat kind where you slide a soda water out of the rack while I wait for somebody to pick me up. The attendant looks at me kind of strange. And I ask him how he knows the man in the black suit, but he says nothing. Then, after I eat a peppermint patty, peanuts, and some orange peanut butter crackers, Emmitt pulls up in his white Rambler.

"Oh Gregory," he says when I get in. "What have you done?"

"Nothing," I say.

"Well the, what has been done to you?"

I take my time telling Emmitt, and he shakes his head. And after I'm through with my story, I feel like I can't talk to Emmitt. So I just answer him "yes" and "no."

I had taken the bus that day, and so I ask Emmitt just to take me to the bus stop so I can catch it home. But he says he will get me home. When he pulls up in front of my house, he turns to me and says, "Gregory, be careful around Mr. White."

"Yes, sir?"

"Do you want me to explain anything to your parents?"

"No sir."

"Do you want to play tennis again?"

I feel myself smile. "Yes, sir," I say. Emmitt's old eyes look kind of watery to me, and he smiles, reaches across the seat, and pats my shoulder as I get out.

When I get out of the old Rambler, my father comes out of the house, looks at me, and says, "What you done?" And I turn from him to wave bye to Emmitt, who is waving rapidly to me from inside his Rambler.

* * *

I was lucky in that incident, but I proved to me and some others that I could hold my own. And people heard, and I got treated better. My mother and father talked to me more, asked me what I had decided to do with myself, asked if they could help me with whatever it was I had decided to do with myself. Mr. White didn't show up for several weeks. Some said he was hiding out, taking it on the lam. And of course, people knew who Fred Carrasco was. The tellers teased me, but they also sort of pampered me, gave me candy, bought me lunch from their homes. Hank Worley pumped me for as much information as he could get from me.

On the weekends, I played tennis with Emmitt, and I once even beat him a set. I saw our games as getting me in shape. So pretty soon it is August, and I know that I got to make some decisions. My future was running toward me. There was the draft, college, and my confusion. Emmitt voted for college and studying economics. He told me had friends at San Antonio College, said he would help me apply. He also told me that he hated to see me go to that nasty war. But then, Mr. White comes back to the bank and then to see me.

It is closing time for the bank, and since Emmitt starts to trust me more, I'm in the vault counting the money by myself. The bars and the timed door are open and in walks Mr. White. I turn and just see him, and my shoulders jump up to my ears. "Gregory," he says. "I owe you, and despite what some people say, I pay my debts."

"Mr White. I got your car blown up, so you really don't owe me nothing."

Mr. White shakes his head, then stares down at his shiny, ostrich skin boots. He takes his LBJ hat off with his right hand and puts it on top of the long row of steel drawers. He straightens out his tie, checks behind him, and keeps his left hand behind his back, like he's holding on to his ass. "Now, Gregory, a boy like you has a future with a fella like me. And I can watch out for your welfare."

"Yes sir. I like it just fine at the bank. I think I want to be a banker."

"I'm not talking about the bank," he says and checks around behind him again. He pulls his left hand from around his back. He's got this little travel case. He reaches in it and pulls out a Steves Bank money sack with what looks like a stack of bills inside. He puts it on the counter next to his hat. He reaches in again. He pulls out four sacks. "I know a lot of people. And from what I have heard about the way you operated around those tough vatos tried to intimidate me, well, I think you could make some money for me and yourself."

"How did you hear about what happened?"

"I know some birds. My wife also says good things." I stare at my toes. "Now these safes and such are filled with old money, right?"

"Schedule to be burned. That's what Emmitt tells me."

"Well then, what would be the harm of exchanging these bags of money for some of them that's in the safe?"

"Oh, I don't think so."

"You can count it. It's the same amount. No one's to know."

"Sir," I say and wish Emmitt is around.

"Like I say. You got a future, but it ain't here. You don't want to be a banker. Bankers hold other people's money."

"But you're a banker."

"I know people on the draft board, politicians, lawyers." He stares at me. I say nothing. "For my wife's sake, let's just exchange one sack for another." Looking at me, he grabs a fifteen-year-old sack of twenties. He puts his sack in its place, then reshuffles the sacks of money, and I let him. Then he stuffs another one of his sacks into the safe. After he is done, he comes to me and pats my shoulder. "You're a good man, Gregory."

"I ain't so good."

"Why don't you call the Feds tell them we got some money to burn. Tell them they should come by and pick it up."

"Emmitt usually makes that call."

"Why don't you do it?" And he stands there patting my shoulder, making me know I will do what he says, and I am mad at him and envious-like of him at the same time.

* * *

By the time that summer was over, I'd go right into Sammy's office. He'd close the door, and we'd discuss my future. He made calls and sent me out to interviews with friends of his. The guy he chose for me to work for was this redheaded, south side, "salesman." When Davy Wolf saw me and talked to me on my interview, he said, "Now with your looks and smooth talk, you can sell some Mexicans some refrigerators." So I did.

I sold refrigerators, cars, air conditioners, whatever Davy Wolf could find, to poor, scared illegals dodging immigration, ones just like Emilio and Tristina. Then Davy showed me the "horse" business. We'd go around to country horse auctions, buy the sick or old ones, and hire an acquaintance to truck them up to Canada where horse meat was legal. Short of it was, I became a salesman like Davy Wolf. Then I got drafted.

With my banking and sales experience, I became a paymaster at Da Nang. The biggest danger I had was from the black soldiers who wanted to beat the shit out of most white non-commissioned officers, especially paymasters. I talked my way to safety. And thinking like Sammy White and Davy Wolf, I found ways to pay myself a little extra.

When I got back, I resumed my career as a salesman and, with Sammy White's help, charged forward into my future or fate. I made more money than any banker, so I guess that I owed Sammy White, who eventually did some prison time. And I figure I never missed much by not going to college. And I guess I didn't miss much by not becoming a banker. But I figure I missed a lot by not keeping up my Saturday tennis games with ol' Emmitt.

Divorce Laws

The Gulf breeze catches the pleasant smell of Kay Menger's freshly cut and sprinkled grass and blows it through the window of my new Toyota pickup, parked inconspicuously down the street from Kay's place. From the full summer moon and the streetlamp on the corner, I can see that Kay Menger's front yard looks like the yards of the other recent divorcees. With no one to help and less time for the house, the ex-wives whom I watch let the yards grow shaggy and fill with their kids' toys.

On my first pass by Kay's house, just before dusk, I saw muddy Ninja warriors and G.I. Joes lying in the lawn's bare spots. The toy soldiers still lie there, in the dark, wounded in action or hiding and waiting for an enemy. The youngest's tricycle with its bent frame and misaligned handlebars is still parked under the pecan tree where he left it. The pecan tree's branches droop from the weight of its sour-smelling ripening pecans and nearly touch the ground. The hedges need trimming, and the awning needs painting. A bit of anxiety about the appearance of the place and what the married neighbors think might creep into Kay's crowded mind once in a while. But, Kay is probably too preoccupied with making a living and caring for the boys now that the hubby is gone to let neighbors' thoughts weigh in the balance of her decisions.

But her grass is cut. A BMW is in the driveway. The suspected boyfriend, the man who brings consolation for the loss of a man, had probably come over for Sunday afternoon. Hoping the two boys would take an afternoon nap so that he and Kay might have a little afternoon delight, he had probably caught Kay's hints, as thoughts about the neighbors and the neighborhood crept into her mind, and mowed the lawn.

The porch light comes on, and the front door opens. I take off my old Stetson fedora, put it beside me, and scoot down in my seat until I can just barely see over the dash of my Toyota pickup. A man, clearly not Mr. Menger, steps out of the door and into the porch light. He has no shoes on;

he carries those in his hand; and his shirt is unbuttoned. Kay Menger stays in the doorway, and the porch light makes her negligee translucent and shows off the trim figure of the thirtyish woman. With a body like hers, I can see why her soon to be ex would just naturally expect boyfriends. The man leans toward her, and she steps up to him. What starts out as a good night peck turns into a full tongue-in-the-throat kiss. They wrap their arms around each other, and he leans her back against the door frame. His hand lowers to her butt. I raise my camera and take the shot. Then, Kay pulls away from him and smiles.

He doesn't want to leave, but he has to. She can't risk his staying. Came over for Sunday dinner, right after going to church with his family. Stayed the afternoon. Stayed through *Sixty Minutes*, then through Sunday night prime time. Stayed until the kids were in bed. And now, he wants desperately to stay in order to pretend this relationship is the way he wished it was. Kay Menger, though, probably suspects that somebody is watching.

The man steps down a few steps, turns, and smiles at Kay. She raises one flat palm to her lips and blows him a kiss. He turns away and starts to walk down the sidewalk, but he suddenly raises one foot, grabs it, and starts hopping on the other foot. A wounded, neglected Ninja warrior, hiding and waiting, had gouged Kay's boyfriend with his sword. The boyfriend turns to face Kay again. She giggles. Then, he gets into his BMW. I take another picture.

I wait until Kay's boyfriend is well down the block before I put on the old Stetson, start my Toyota pickup, and leave Kay to her dreams. It was an amicable divorce until Kay's lawyer told her to ask for the kids, a sizeable chunk of child support, and half of her husband's retirement and savings. So, her husband got Mike Cronin and thus me to help him out. Now Kay will be lucky to get the kids.

Chain smoking, hyper-tense, happily married Mike Cronin is the meanest, toughest divorce lawyer in Austin, Texas. Since my own divorce from Victoria and resulting poverty and underemployment, Mike Cronin hires me to find nasty facts for highly contested divorces. What God joined together, Mike Cronin and I can put asunder. Mike uses my research only if he needs it; he likes to have it ready if the proceedings get ugly. He is expensive, but in court, his clients usually beat the shit out of their ex-spouses. Back when I tried to be a hippie, I believed in free love, but now I know it's never free.

But for now, on this Sunday night, as the suburbanites settle in for another hard week, sneak a peek at their cute kids sleeping, or silently hump in their bedrooms, I snake through their neighborhood like a premonition of their futures. I smell their freshly cut and sprinkled carpet grass in the gentle Gulf breeze. It smells like their failing dreams.

* * *

Divorced, living alone, staring at the dark ceiling of my bachelor pad, I find myself unable to quit thinking. I need a little sympathy. But Victoria, of course, isn't around, and Sally Carpenter, the legal secretary I sometimes date, a poor substitute for a lover, is at home worried about her kids and bills and ex-husband.

On our first date, Sally Carpenter told me that she just wasn't ready for a "real date." Her divorce was too recent, and she wondered what her two kids, a five-year-old boy and a nine-year-old girl, would think of her seeing somebody other than their daddy. From across the table she held my hand, then quickly let it go. We mostly watched the rain on the window outside of the restaurant. Finally, she asked me if I would take her home.

Since there were still places to go on a Saturday night, I sat in a bar on Sixth Street. And due to some strange luck, I met a nineteen-year-blonde coed. She had gotten far too drunk and gotten separated from her friends. She was complimented that someone as old as me would buy her another drink and try to help her find her friends. When we couldn't find her friends, she perhaps began to think her drunkenness was excuse enough to let me get into her pants. In the future, she would perhaps tell her sorority sisters and later her girlfriends, maybe even her husband, about the wild drunken night she spent with a dirty old man. This wasn't like love either, but the youth and exuberance of the wild-eyed girl, happy as hell at being out of a small West Texas town and committing real sin, was enough to give me a weekend of undisturbed sleep.

Kay Menger is probably happily asleep now. But because I saw her with her boyfriend, she soon won't be able to sleep either. Maybe, like me, late at night, she'll go to one of the Jim's Restaurants, and have a cup of coffee and a breakfast taco. I can still taste the taco.

As I roll around on my bed, plant my face into the pillow, then hold the pillow over my face, I remember and think about back then. Good times were easier to have then, back when I was in college and had met Victoria. At times, I am almost amused at what I thought mattered. Then, in love with Victoria, with a joint and a few beers, I fancied myself some crusader for the new age of enlightenment. But now I spy on Kay Menger, and I know that we are still in some dark age.

I get up and walk around my dark apartment, using memory rather than sight. If I turn on my lights, maybe I could gain sight and lose memory. Could I sleep with the lights on? But now, memory has control over me and will make me sleepy and grumpy the next day. Fortunately, all I have to do is visit Mike and deliver the photos of Kay and her boyfriend. I'll have to catch up on my sleep tomorrow night.

A new job would help. I do have a dated law degree. Mike sometimes mentions making me a partner. I have other contacts. I do a little of Austin's real estate law business. Austin is full of greedy landlords with roach infested, crumbling student ghettos. So, I post ads around campus, and UT students read my ads and hire me to get their property deposits back or sue for their damaged personal goods. Nothing goes to court, but I get $25 for a one-page, threatening letter, $35 for a visit, and $50 to go see the sons of bitches who lease the places. But these ventures do not pay my own alimony and child support. My sixteen-year-old daughter needs Reebok tennis shoes, Guess jeans, Nintendo games, and a drawer full of her mail-ordered make up. Evidently she does not need the books I buy for her. She never reads them. No, Mike Cronin pays for my family's needs.

I think about my upstairs neighbor. George played tackle and linebacker next to Tommy Nobis for the '63 and '64 Longhorns. He is still an old-school jock, from a time even before the real sixties, when football was not the way to fame or fortune, but still something resembling a game. He has the easy grace and humor of a jock, and also a jock's simplicity. "I thought it would be easy," he told me one night when I joined him for a beer. "You come home after work. You buy the little boys toy soldiers and toy guns; you buy the little girls dolls. Now none of it works." He had to be a success in life to support his former wives and houses. Tonight is for thought.

* * *

My feet slap the red-graveled, soggy running path and splatter pools of water. It is the day after a rain, and the weather is clear but humid. I ought to move west to a drier climate. Sweat pastes my shorts to my legs today. Beads of it run down from my forehead and into my eyes and mouth. I blink against the salty sting and blow the bitter taste out of my mouth. I hope for a second wind to make this all easier, but none comes.

The woman whom I recognize as the "oriental coed" chugs by me in her choppy, studied jogging style. She nods her head, and I smile as best I can. In the past, I have thought about changing directions and joining her, striking up a conversation, but she wears a Walkman, and I doubt if she would pull the plugs out of her ears just for a conversation with an aging hippie jogger.

As I jog, I recognize other joggers who run by me or, because of a stronger kick, pass me. When we meet, I raise my hand in a lazy wave, or nod my head. My soggy footfalls join the chorus of running shoes hitting the pea gravel of the Austin Parks and Recreation Dept.'s jogging/hiking/biking trails that run alongside the Colorado River and Barton Creek.

We aren't running away from anything or running toward some-thing, we just run. If asked why we run, we would shrug our shoulders and say, "It helps me relax, clears my head, or feels good when I quit." Better than smoking marijuana. So we run and take pride in flattened bellies, tightened asses, and bulging calves.

Later today, I'll have to go to a bank and try to con a teller who knows Mike Cronin into letting me see the deposits that Terry Delouche has made over the past six months. Mrs. Delouche thinks that her husband is lying about just how much money he has coming in from his computer consultancy firm and wants her fair share, which is all she can get. From the bank, I must drive to Bonham Junior High, and find Suzie and Billy Sandoval as they walk home from school. Mrs. Sandoval hired some other lawyer than Mike Cronin when she got her divorce, so she lost her two kids. Now she wants them back. She suspects Mr. Sandoval of child abuse. So, she has hired Mike Cronin and me to get her kids back. I must ask Suzie and Billy delicate questions about their lives with their dad.

I will give each kid $20 and charge Mike Cronin.

I chug up the steps of a bridge and cross to the other side of Barton Creek. Why do I jog? Why does the question keep coming up when I jog? In the sixties, we wanted to be in good spiritual shape. Now, we want to boast that we still have the same size waists that we had back when we wanted a spiritual workout.

I finish my jog at Deep Eddy pool. I pull off my new $80 New Balance jogging shoes, the type Mike Cronin calls sneakers, and my sweaty ankle high socks, stuff them into my shoes, put the shoes under a picnic table, and take a running dive into the chilly spring water of Deep Eddy Pool. I surface and feel my heart thump from being first hot then chilly. The lifeguard, a UT student, blows his whistle at me, yells, "Don't run," then smiles. From the water, I wave, nod my head, and he smiles and waves back. It is a routine that we go through on the days when I take my dip at Deep Eddy's. The admonition is mainly for show, for the early morning kids and his boss.

I start a breast stroke and then change into a crawl as I get halfway across the pool. Why do I jog then dive into this pool? Because it feels good. Because I still can do it. Because I can do it in this part of the country. I catch up with the older lady in the baggy black swimming suit and bathing cap. She is finishing her daily morning laps. She does a few more in the evening. She hits the bank, expertly curls, and starts back across the pool. I have yet to perfect the curl. I get water up my nose and come up coughing. So I grab the cement lip, tuck my feet up under me, and push off from the side of the pool. I start swimming as fast as I can, and the older lady, use to our game, sensing I'm gaining on her, starts to stroke harder. I ease up as I get to the opposite bank to let her win. She hoists herself up on to the bank and smiles at me. "Why don't you race somebody your own size and weight," she says to me.

"They're no competition," I say. Someday we should introduce ourselves to each other.

She pulls off her bathing cap and starts to towel off. I have no towel, so I walk back to the picnic table, my feet getting muddy once I step off the cement that surrounds the pool. The young lifeguard yells again, "No more running, or we'll kick you out." The threat sounds good. The children stare up at him with their wide eyes. Their mothers point up to him and whisper to their children, "See there." The lifeguard turns his attention away from me and returns his attention to the pool, but he holds his chin a little higher. I like my role as the bad example. In running to the pool and diving in, I perform a social function; I fulfill my civic duty. Same as in my job.

I lie down on the picnic table and look up, through the branches of the pecan tree that shades me, at the blue sky and the sun's glare. I squint to make the sun hazy. I close my eyes to stare at the orange backsides of my eyelids. Why do I jog, especially after a sleepless night?

While I jog, I think. The increased motion increases thought, and I seem to work through so much. I do my wondering about Kay Menger. I do my planning for my rounds for the day. I remember my wife and kid, retrace our history, ponder my decisions and actions, punish myself for my mistakes, question myself about what was a mistake and what was not, suggest to myself that the whole outcome was inevitable.

No more thought, though. The thoughts I build up during sleepless nights are used up in jogging the next morning. I have taken my plunge into the cold water and feel relaxed and drained. It is time for a morning nap under the pecan, cottonwoods, and Cypress around Deep Eddy Pool. But it occurs to me that with my skills I could ruin the life of any of my acquaintances on the jogging paths or at Deep Eddy Pool.

* * *

I wait outside Mike Cronin's office, my legs crossed, the photos of Kay Menger in a manilla folder resting on my lap, my hat on top of the folder. Mike's secretary, an older lady wearing half-frame glasses with a gold chain connected to their arms and running around her neck, lowers her head to peer at me. She smiles. I pull the photos out from under the hat and raise them, "Someday, I'm going to catch you Betty," I say. And Betty lets a sly smile slip into one corner of her mouth. She drops her head as I lower the photos back into my lap.

"If I were foolin' around, I wouldn't get caught, and I'd make damn sure my husband didn't get Mike Cronin for a lawyer," Betty says, her head still down. She sorts through the mail and keeps her stoic, straight face on. I am glad that Betty is in Mike's office. Sometimes, I think that Mike keeps her as his only secretary so that he isn't tempted by more innocent, less grouchy, younger women.

The door to Mike Cronin's office opens and a well dressed brunette steps out. Mike is right behind her. She turns her head to look at me, and I stand and nod my head out of the "graciousness" that my mother pounded into me and law school reinforced.

As I smile at her, we let our eyes linger on each other, perhaps attracted to each other, perhaps just curious. I note that she wears a navy blue business suit, the classy and sexless uniform of a professional woman. But this professional's blouse plunges lower than a man's shirt, to reveal plenty of cleavage. The tight skirt stretches over a rounded butt that is still youthful but may develop into a middle-aged spread without dieting and exercise. Dark eyes under the lighter hair and slightly up-turned nose make her pretty and almost girlish. Mike will probably tell her to keep the cleavage and the tight skirt out of court. When she turns back to Mike, I notice that the mascara and rouge under one eye is slightly smeared. She had probably started to cry, and Mike had probably consoled her with his "gracious" manner that he learned not from law school, not from his mother, but from twenty-two years as a divorce lawyer. When you pay for Mike Cronin, you get all the extras.

Mike shakes her hand, says "goodbye," but does not introduce her to me. What I now do for a living surrounds me with women, many real stunners, all lonely and hoping for or susceptible to anybody willing to show some "graciousness." But what I do for a living only lets me watch. I can't touch them, rarely talk to them; I never see the results of my work.

Mike and I watch as she walks out the front door. Betty lifts her head to watch us watching. I wink at her. She returns to her work. Mike lightly slaps me with the back of his hand and jerks his head toward his office. I grab my photos and put my hat on. We go into his office, and Mike walks behind his desk, sits down, and leans back in his high, plush office chair. Mike's cream colored chair matches his peach colored walls, which is a good color to highlight Mike's rounded ceramic sculptures and shiny split rocks. The interior decorator who bought the sculptures, painted the walls, and moved the furniture around says it's a good color.

"Jesus," Mike says and lets his cream colored chair spring him forward, "I can smoke with you." He quickly reaches into his desk drawer and pulls out his pack of cigarettes. He pulls one out and illegally lights up.

Since Mike's building adopted a no smoking policy, Mike is having hell not smoking around his clients. He could get kicked out of the building for filling other peoples' lungs with his smoke. Another irony thatthe passage of time creates is that the earth mothers and health freaks who came out of the sixties turned into health fascists making sure you say "no."

"Whatever happened to the American and God-given right to destroy yourself in your own manner," Mike says, inhales, and smiles at me. "Jesus fucking Christ," he says, "you're not in college anymore, you don't live on a ranch anymore, and the sixties are over. You don't have to still dress in Levis and sneakers. Get you a pair of slacks. And, if you have to wear a hat, get something besides that thing." Mike inhales and holds in the smoke.

I take my hat off, hold it up so that both Mike and I can see it, and I say, "This is a good hat, broken in, distinct." Then, I prop one foot on Mike's desk. "These 'sneakers' cost me $80."

"Get some class Roger," Mike says with smoke coming out of his nostrils. I lift my foot off of his desk and put my hat in my lap.

"I left all my class in college." I throw the manila folder on his desk. "This should prove I got no class."

"You get a pair of slacks, couple of sportcoats, a business suit, and I might make you a partner." Mike starts to open the envelope.

"Why the hell would I want to give up this great job? I set my own hours, get to look at nasty pictures, spy on pillars of the community."

"Well, yeah," Mike says as he dangles his cigarette out of his mouth and looks at the first 8 x 10 glossy. "But somebody's got to do it." He looks at me, "That's why I hire you to do it." He chuckles while a cloud of smoke wraps around his head.

"So what do you think? Am I getting better with the camera?"

Mike stands, "You're a goddamn artist. Keep your sneakers. You're genius. Look at the well placed shadows adding drama. Look at the stark beams of lights, invoking the work of Walker Evans. Look at the emotion in those faces." Mike slaps the back of his hand against the glossy.

I rise and put my hat on. "Well, I've got some more 'art' to do. Some other lawyers like my pictures. And, I've got some of my own cases."

Mike lowers the photos for a moment, "You've got your own cases?"

"Mostly U.T. students."

"Shit," Mike says and looks back at the photo, "So you're writing nasty letters to landlords at $20 a pop."

"Some of the student-exploiting, bourgeoisie pigs might actually go to court."

"For a $75 property deposit that the student probably doesn't deserve back anyway? Who is going to take the trouble? Keep writing your letters."

"Weirder things have happened."

"Well, be sure to give me credit for inspiration and understanding in your memoirs."

"Thanks, Mike," I say as I reach for the door to his office.

"Roger," Mike says as I step into his doorway. I turn to listen. "You really are good at this, seriously. I've never seen anybody catch on so quick, build up so many contacts so fast." Then a smile comes back to Mike's mouth. He slaps his hands together, " We've got Kay Menger by the short hairs."

"Great Mike, give her a tug for me," I say.

"Pervert," Mike says. "Get out of here. Go make us some money."

* * *

Green Pastures is probably the poshest eatery in Austin. Peacocks spread their tails and cry out, sounding like terrified or tortured infants. I push the old Stetson back on my head and absorb the shade as I walk under Green Pastures' tall oaks. My $80 NB's sink into the thick lawn that is damn near an overly thick carpet. Green Mansions has a landscaping consultant. The restaurant itself is an old Edwardian mansion with a Texas-style porch completely surrounding it. It is the type of high-ceilinged, spacious, shaded home that was built in Texas before air conditioning changed architecture and aesthetics. It too is now air conditioned. Inside, during serving hours, young waiters don't hand out menus but write the day's servings in French on black slate boards, black not green like modern day "black" boards, with yellow and blue chalk. As they meticulously make the loops of their neat script, they pronounce the French dishes for you, so if you listen close, you can order without sounding like a Texan. It is all sort of intimidating. I've known the owner and the business manager since Victoria worked at The Green Pastures as a waitress.

I go to the backdoor, as Dominique instructed, and knock. The beefy kitchen manager with the trim beard and coiffured hair opens the door and holds it open for me, "Can I help you?"

"Yes, I'm here to see Dominique," I say and take off my hat.

The manager steps back and says, "So you're the guy he mentioned." I shrug my shoulders. "Just as well you caught me, I'm the guy you really need to see. Why don't you come into the office."

"Well, its sort of a private matter," I say.

"Hey, this is a classy joint. Lot of people wanting to work here. And cause you know Dominique. . ."

I interrupt, "No. You don't understand. I'm not here. . ."

The manager is just as determined to interrupt me. "You're gonna have to start out washing dishes. Your hair is a little long, but I don't think you'll need a net. Then, we'll put you out on the floor. Course, you might need some better duds, but we've got an arrangement for that."

Why does every third person worry about the way I dress? Willy Nelson makes a fashion statement, and I'm labeled a bum. "No, I'm not here for a job." I try again. "Well, really I'm here to do my job."

The manager rubs his beard. "What is your job?"

"I'm an investigator," I say and step through the door.

The manager closes the door behind me and says, "A cop, huh?"

"A private investigator."

I continue to walk, and the manager sidesteps to keep up with me, "Like Spencer, Jim Rockford, Mannix, right?"

"Just like them," I say.

"You don't look much like those guys."

"They don't look much like me." I enjoy our game, but I'm in a hurry and want to get my business with Dominique over. "Where is Dominique?"

"Follow me, Marlow," the manager says, and I follow him into the dining area. Inside, Green Pastures is not as plush as the plants outside. It has clean walls with authentic-looking wallpaper and old portraits, lots of space and light, wooden tables with lace tablecloths, and gleaming silver forks, spoons, and knives.

Dominique sits at a table, his fingers curled, checking his nails.

"Thank you," I say to the manager.

"You're welcome Kojak," he says, giggles, then adds, "No, he's a real cop."

"And, I'm an unreal guy," I say.

I walk to Dominique's table, and he immediately hops up and gestures to a chair across the table from him. I pull the chair out from under the table and sit. Dominique reaches across the table to shake my hand. I am careful not to harm his manicure. Dominique, of course, is not his real name. He is a Chicano from Laredo, but after flunking out of UT, he purchased the clothes, the haircuts, and the cosmetics to pass himself off as European. From what I'd seen in the movies, I'd say he gives the place a hint of the Riviera. "Well, Mr. Jackson, so glad to meet you again."

"My pleasure," I say. The Laredo kid also worked on his pronunciation (suggesting East European rather than Texas Spanish) and his manners. He came to me because his landlord evicted him. I wrote a letter, which did him no good (he was guilty as hell of catching his landlord's sofa on fire), but I got him an interview at Green Pastures because another "client" washed dishes. Dominique took to Green Pastures more than studying, so he became "Dominique" and worked his way up to maitre'd. Reputedly, he took no notes, wrote nothing down, would remember every guest's name, their reservation time, and preferred table. He was a success story. He had put his intelligence to work for him and was doing something useful for his society. He owed me.

Dominique put his elbows on the table and leaned across it toward me. "Mr. Howard Bigelow was in here just last night."

"This is not top secret," I said to Dominique. "We can relax."

"Sure," Dominique said. "You want a coke or something? I can even get you a beer."

"No thank you," I said. "Back to 'Senator' Bigelow," I said.

"Wow, Jesus, the vato is a fucking senator?" the Laredo boy asked.

"A state senator, and some of his constituents back in West Texas want to know how he's spending their money and with whom. The legislature has been out of session for a month, and no one can account for Senator Bigelow."

"Yeah Rog, I see what you're getting at," Dominique says. "He was with a real fox. Thirty at the most. Jewelry. Boobs to here. My guess was

120

first that she's some kind of society lady. But, a waiter thinks maybe she's some kind of high class hooker. Good stuff, huh? Am I going to read about this in the papers?"

"How long was he here?"

"Three hours, man."

"Did he drink much?"

"A bottle of champagne an hour."

"How much was his bill?"

"Two hundred and nine dollars and seventy-six cents," Dominique says, proud of his memory.

I reach across the table and pat Dominique's shoulder. "Maybe you ought to go into partnership with me."

"Shit, Rog, you know what I make in tips?"

I reach into my pocket, pull out the crisp $50 bill that Jim Sledge gave me, and handed it to Dominique. "Tip for a tip," I say. Jim Sledge is the Big Spring lawyer working for Mrs. Senator Bigelow. I went to school with the state representative from Big Spring who is thinking about running for Senator Bigelow's seat, and he recommended me to Jim Sledge.

Dominique holds up the bill. "Yeah, same as what Senator Bigelow tipped the waiter," he says.

I scoot my chair back and say, "If he makes another reservation, why don't you give me a call and make me a reservation for the same time. Better yet, fifteen minutes later, but get me a table close by."

"You need a date too?" he asks.

"I'll try to get my own, but I may need the house coat and tie," I say. I stand, we shake hands, and Dominique shows me out the front door. I put on my hat and walk across the wooden porch.

"Nice hat," Dominique says.

"Thanks. It's old and authentic," I say over my shoulder as I go down the front steps.

I step into the cool shade of the oak trees. I turn to wave goodbye to Dominique. He returns my wave, smiles, then crosses his fingers. I stick my hands into the pockets of my Dickie khakis. I remember picking Victoria up after a hard night of waiting tables. We sat in the dark under the trees while she rubbed her bare feet in the soft grass. We kissed and fondled each other, and her manager yelled out at us to stop. "This is not goddamn lovers' lane," he said. Today is a good day for me. I've probably helped right a social wrong, have probably ruined another marriage (Mrs. Bigelow is one of the concerned constituents), and have probably gotten a free meal at Green Pastures (Jim Sledge, of course, will pick up my tab).

* * *

Betty sits behind her typewriter, stares through her half-framed glasses at the document she is supposedly proofreading, lightly rocks in her squeaking swivel chair, and pretends not to be trying to hear what goes on in Mike Cronin's office. I sit across from Betty, smile at her, to try to break her pretense, and listen myself for some distinct meaningful sound, something other than the low grumble of voices coming from behind Mike's closed door. I have no real reason for being here, but just for once, I want to see the result of my "work."

Mike's door slowly creaks open, and an arm with a lawyer's blue, pin-striped suit sleeve wrapped around it holds the door open for Kay Menger. She comes through the door with her head hung down. She is trying to keep more tears from running down her cheek and staining the collar of her white blouse. Her eyes seem to have sunken farther into her skull, leaving shadows around them. She too wears a suit. Next, Kay's lawyer, Fred C. Wemple, comes through the door. Kay has not chosen well; Fred C. Wemple's name is a good name for a lawyer like him. And I can see from his drooping jowls and shoulders, his fake smile, the way he hesitantly touches the elbow of his client that Fred C. Wemple has just gotten his ass kicked.

Mike Cronin doesn't smile. He has done this enough to know just the right officious look to hide any gloating, smugness, or victory elation that he might feel. He is as classy an act as he can be given his job. Mr. Kay Menger does smile, way too broadly. The kind of taunting smile a jock would smile after he has caught the touchdown pass and wants to point the nose of ball at the defender he has just beaten. He too wears a suit.

I grab my hat and stand as Ms. Kay Menger walks in front of me. She stops to look at me. "I'm the guy who took the pictures," I say. "I am sorry." This admission is why I came. It makes all the pieces fit, shows all the hands. Kay Menger will hurt some more, but at least I can give her the whole truth, the way reality lurked around with me in my cab and then bit her in the ass. Now at least she need not wonder where she went wrong.

She looks around her. First at her lawyer, Fred C. Wemple, and he can offer no support, no advice, next at her soon-to-be-former husband, who only smiles some more, next at Mike, who looks at me like I've lost my mind. Even Betty looks at me.

I twirl the old Stetson in my hands. "How can you ruin people's lives?" Kay Menger asks me. Inside Mike Cronin's private office, Fred C. Wemple talked for her. Outside, with me, where she can be "unofficial," she can put her confusion and anger into words. This too I give her.

"Someone leaves you, or you leave someone, and your life will be ruined. At least for awhile. With or without someone like me," I tell her, and Mike Cronin rushes past me to Kay and tries to lead her out of his office.

"Ms. Menger," I say, and Kay looks at me. "I'm not really sorry for what I did, but I am sorry." Kay turns away from Mike to look at me. "Do you understand at all?"

She stares at me for just a moment. It is a blank stare, as though Kay's mind cannot work fast enough to deal with me, the lawyers, the photos, and a ruined life. Her eyebrows knit as she tries to speak. She is desperate. She wants to hurt somebody. Here, outside Mike's official office, she can. She looks down at my hat. "That's an ugly hat."

I look down at my hat as Mike leads the whole party to his office door. As they file out, I walk into Mike's peach and cream colored office and sit in one of the three padded chairs in front of his desk.

Mike comes in and says, "Jesus, Roger. You gone soft, crazy, addled?"

Mike takes off his coat and throws it on the conference table across from his desk. He hooks his index finger over the knot of his tie and pulls at his shirt collar. He sits down as I explain, "Seems I finally did the least I could do."

Mike reaches into his front drawer and pulls out a pack of cigarettes and fumbles with it as he pulls out a cigarette and puts it between his lips. "Now she'll probably tell her neighbors, and you won't be able to drive any place in town without people pulling their kids inside and closing their blinds."

Next, Mike reaches into a deeper, longer drawer and pulls out a bottle of scotch and two glasses. He pours both of us a drink, scoots a filled glass close to me, sips his scotch, then lights his cigarette. "What the hell, huh? She gets to keep the kids but loses the house, and nobody goes before a judge."

"Happy ever after," I say.

"Doesn't get any easier," Mike says as a curve of smoke wraps around his head. A vein in his neck seems to push against his buttoned up shirt. Another vein stands out in his forehead as though big spurts of blood gush through it. He's probably due for his first heart attack.

I sip my scotch and get ready to bullshit with Mike in order to help him celebrate and calm down. Mike and I are in the truth business. We ferret it out and then hold it up in front of the faces of the innocent, and if they refuse to recognize the truth, Mike pushes their noses into it. Then, when we can, we leave our jobs and go back to our own fantasies.

Massage Therapy

Haley heard the pounding at the door and the word, *police.* Her mind blotted out all the other sounds. She looked from the bed to the window and remembered that they were on the second floor of the Economy Motel. As her mind raced ahead, then jumped back, then forward, it stuck for a moment on a number: her lawyer's cell phone. Then another number kept her mind from racing: Roger's cell.

She knew this moment could come. Everyone at the Golden Day Massage Parlor knew that this could happen. Haley looked toward the door and saw her lawyer, naked except for his underwear and socks, trying to pull his pants, shirts, and jacket from the closet. Like so many others, Frank had kept his socks on during the whole session. She chuckled. But maybe she ought to call him. She imagined his phone ringing in his slacks' pocket, adding to his panic, while he struggled to put his legs into his pants, he could dig through his knotted pockets to retrieve his cell phone, answer it, and she could ask: "Frank, what would your legal advice be?" Haley knew that this could happen, perhaps was bound to happen. Yet, she couldn't make it upset her. She couldn't get concerned, so she chuckled.

"Just a moment," Frank Longley yelled toward the door. But the door slammed open, and a petite woman police officer was the first in the room. Haley pulled the bed sheet up to her chest and looked squarely at the lady cop whose eyes under the police cap visor darted like a robot's to follow the barrel of her pistol. Haley continued to laugh. And while the police woman's fellow officers filed in behind her and the housekeeper who had let them in eyed the scene from the hallway, the police woman's eyes settled on Haley. Haley could not stop her laughing. Obviously, with Haley's solid laughter floating around the room, infecting Frank so that he stared shaking from suppressing his chuckle, no one would start shooting. The housekeeper laughed. The police woman lowered her pistol, but the officer kept her eyes on Haley. The lady tilted her head to get her cap's brim out of her line of sight and smiled, and then, in some sort of communion or recognition with Haley, started laughing along with Haley. No matter what the moralists said, this scene, though played a thousand times a day across the country, was funny. And Haley could not get the funniness of it out of her head.

Frank had gotten his pants on but not his shirt, and he held his tie, in a loosened knot so that he could slip it over his head, in his left hand. "This isn't what it looks like," he said. Haley laughed some more. It was exactly what it looked like.

"It never is," the soft-faced cop said. Haley laughed harder. The woman cop laughed.

"Officer Henderson," a male police officer said to scold the lady cop. But the lady kept laughing, holstered her pistol, and stepped toward Haley.

"You have the right to remain silent . . ." another cop began to intone.

When the cop had finished telling Frank and Haley their rights, Haley asked, "Do you think that I could get dressed?"

"Do you have anything to put on?" Officer Henderson asked.

Haley, with her hands still holding her sheet to the tops of her shoulders, motioned with her hand to the closet. "You better start dressing," Officer Henderson said. "We can't turn our backs."

Haley, thinking that her laughter and amusement had made this a performance, folded her sheet off of her, stood, stretched, slowly walked to the closet, then just as slowly reached to the hanger for her clothes. "Excuse me," Henderson said. Then added, "Mam," and gestured toward the bathroom. Without slipping into panties or bra, Haley took exaggerated, long steps toward the bathroom. She wanted to show the males what Frank had paid for. When she stepped inside, Henderson closed the door. Now, backstage, in her dressing room, Haley looked at her dresser, she pulled her strapless bra in place and turned her back to Henderson who hooked it closed for her. "New job?" Haley asked Henderson over her shoulder.

"Six months full time. I was lucky to get this assignment," Henderson said.

Haley turned to face the woman and stepped into her panties.

Henderson couldn't help herself, "You?"

"I've been doing this one way or another for years," Haley said. "Wait, that could be held against me."

"Yes, ma'am. It could."

"But I meant it to be funny. As women, I mean, we all do this. You ought to know, Officer Henderson."

Officer Henderson gritted her teeth, "That'll be enough, Mam. No reason to insult the uniform."

"But I'm not meaning to insult . . ." Haley tsked. "I just mean none of this real. This is a comedy, not a drama."

"Ma'am, your sentence will be real, and it won't be funny."

* * *

The Golden Day was a legitimate massage therapy business. And Haley, who had studied massage, as well as a great many other things, primarily gave massages to old people with their muscles in knots. With warm oil spread on her hands and her client's backs, Haley could manipulate and push the old folks' doughy fat to get underneath to the muscles and stretch them. When she got that deep, an older client would usually clinch her teeth and moan, but then, with the loosening muscle relaxing into a limp rope, the clients would melt. From that point on, it was a pleasure to do her job. Then the massage was like kneading dough. And when the elderly clients would leave with the tingle of the massage still in their backs or limbs, they would work a shoulder or jiggle a hip and smile in appreciation. But no masseuse could make that much money from these loosened, appreciative older folks.

A female masseuse would inevitably get a lewd comment or an offer from the men she massaged. Most virile men just couldn't let loose of the idea of a "massage parlor," the type that used to appear out on interstates and cater to truckers. So Barbara Koons, who managed the Golden Day Massage Therapy, and Haley talked and thought and calculated and came up with the idea of making a counteroffer to the lewd comments made by virile or even the unvirile men. Innuendo led to method. So a gentleman could call and arrange an appointment. And if he asked in the right code, the masseuse or Barbara met him at motel for an afternoon or early evening massage. Word spread, reputation grew, and Haley was soon meeting the needs of some of the more prominent male citizens of Beaumont, Texas. She met male doctors, lawyers, bankers, judges, and professors. In the process, she made enough to pay her tuition and put some money in the bank. She also got lots of legal, medical, financial, and some academic advice. Haley was nine hours short of a degree and had the grades and brains to get into law school. Many of her clients could help her.

As the cops led her out of the motel dressed in her tie-behind, cotton and Tencel blouse with the plunging neckline, off-white twill jeans, and high-heeled flip-flops, but handcuffed—Haley felt the August humidity seize her. She felt beads of sweat form on her face and felt sogginess under her arms and across the strap of her bra, and the cop's hand on the underside of her bicep felt clammy and wet. As Haley and the cops stepped in unison down the metal stairs of the Economy 8 Motel, Haley cussed August Beaumont, just as Roger always did.

Salesmen, a few families with kids, and some motel housekeepers, drifted out of rooms and into the heat, working up their own sweats, to watch Haley being escorted by the cops. Haley had stopped laughing but kept smiling. She had this audience, but with her walk, her head held high, her smile, her blonde hair glowing, her outfit showing she had prepared for this heat, this occasion, she showed them that she was not mortified, not ashamed. And in fact, looking at huffing Henderson with the beads of sweat running off her face, she felt sorry for the officers, who were dressed in black synthetic and cotton uniforms. They must have baked.

Then, feeling self-absorbed, she twisted slightly from the policeman's grip on her upper arm, pulled her head around to see Frank handcuffed, head hanging, shuffling into the story of the defeat of his life and ambitions. Haley shouted. "Are you okay?"

Frank looked up from his escort cop. "Why no. Of course not," he answered.

"Frank, good luck," Haley shouted as she got close to the police car. And as Henderson gently folded her head forward, Haley felt that she was taking a bow to her audience.

* * *

"What tipped us off, Haley, was that there weren't cars at the Golden Day," Henderson said to Haley as she was getting fingerprinted. "I'm Gwen Henderson, by the way," she said to Haley. "We won't have a bail bondsman come around for some time yet, so unless you know someone, you've got a long wait."

"Thank you for your kindness," Haley said. And she paused to look down at the petite Gwen Henderson, who could in Haley's imagination very easily have been a masseuse, and deliberately smiled, just as she had for her attractive mug shot.

"Is that a real smile," Gwen asked.

"Of course, thank you."

"I've had whores try to knife me," Gwen said. "You're confusing."

"This doesn't have to be ugly or humiliating," Haley said.

"But how can it not be?"

Gwen's question required a long answer, and Haley wanted to give it. But the jailers pulled her away from Gwen, and over her shoulder, Haley saw Gwen form a shrug with her body, and Gwen's face drooped into a frown.

In the holding tank, with just one other woman sleeping in a corner, Haley sat on the folding chair and gazed out the fiberglass wall at the wall beyond. She could wait for the bail bondsman to come, but if she waited that long, Roger would worry. Still, she did not want to call him, not yet, she wanted to sit in the quiet holding cell and think before she made her phone call.

Haley thought that Roger, of all people, would surely understand, for Roger was a specialist in human infidelities. He made his living on them. Before he retired to part- time work, Roger made a living taking photos of cheating spouses. Three years before, when she was called to testify at a divorce hearing as the "other woman," the unshaven man, wearing a polo shirt and ironed shorts, who had ducked his eyes from her as he testified about what he had seen, stopped her and apologized for bringing her into the nastiness.

He held his head down as he mumbled his apology to her. He said that he had been doing this for some time and that the view from his digital camera gave him just part of the story. So he wanted to try to make something right.

What Haley did not tell him three years before, what she still had never said to Roger, was that the good husband with her was not having a torrid affair with her but was paying her. The enjoyment or enthusiasm or joy or willingness or maneuvers the good husband couldn't get from his wife, he got from Haley. He still loved his wife, didn't want to lose her, but Roger's photo of Haley and him ended that gentleman's marriage. And this silly man divorced his wife, leaving her to think that he had found another lover, not just someone to give him some loving.

Back, three years before, as Roger mumbled his apology to her, Haley found herself wondering about this late fiftyish man who had not shaved that morning. Despite his stubble, despite his shorts, he was very well-spoken, illustrated his points with examples, did not talk with a discernable Texas accent. He could be charming. So Haley asked for a dinner, then another, and then moved in with Roger. She had done more than moved in with him. She had taken his money. She let him buy her a life. And she thought that she had given him more than simple loving.

The person sleeping on a cot at the other side of the holding cell sat up. It was Dolores. When Dolores saw Haley, she dropped her head into her hands, and Haley heard her say, "Oh, shit." Dolores was a Filipino who worked at the Golden Day also. "You too?" Dolores asked.

"Less than an hour ago."

"My appointment was earlier."

Dolores pushed herself up. She wore very tight shorts and a t-shirt with a plunging V-neck. "You wore those expensive clothes?" Dolores asked.

"Why not? I wasn't going to massage anyone."

"How am I ever going to get my nursing degree now?" Dolores asked.

"Arrests don't get you kicked out of school or the program."

"I mean how am I going to afford it?"

Haley began thinking about the same thing. "Maybe, we should have met them outside of town, or at least in south county."

"So what are you going to do?"

"Maybe there are some openings giving massages just to women."

"So you think somebody would hire us? After this?"

"It was good, quick money. We should have saved more."

The door to the tank opened, and another afternoon criminal joined them, Barbara Koons, the owner of the Golden Day Massage Therapy. "Hello, ladies," Barbra said.

Barbara had a slight cut along the brow of her left eye, and her right eye was puffy. "Barbara, did you fight them?" Haley asked.

"The sons of bitches," Barbara said. "It was a fucking sting. They'd been watching us for several months." Barbara sat beside Haley. She was trying to keep her chin from quivering. "It smells like pee in here," she said.

"You ain't been in here too many times, huh?" Dolores said. "Probably is pee."

"What are you going to do?" Haley asked Barbara.

"I'll take the hardest fall for procurement. I guess I'll lose the business and grow broke."

"Wha, wha," Dolores said. "All you worried about is you."

Haley put her arm around Barbara's shoulders. "We'll all just become trash," Barbara said. She looked at Haley, "I'll bet they looked at you like trash. To them, we'll just be whores."

"Ain't that kind of what we are?" Dolores asked. Dolores stared at the floor and muttered, "I pray every morning and every night. So why is my life so fucked up?"

Haley had been above average in intelligence and looks but poor when she was growing up in East Texas. She sensed that she could do something different with either looks or intelligence, but she had no script; no one had written one for her. So before she ever got out of high school, she developed a certain resignation toward what waited for her and those girls like her. She resisted the usual clichés: an early marriage and/or kid. But she found herself stuck in other clichés dead-end jobs, several semesters of flunked community college courses, and a reputation of being easy. Before Roger, men were fun but not very interesting. So she figured that she might as well get paid for what she saw as giving nothing away. And the money she got for what she did not give away, she reinvested in herself: a good dentist, a touched-up nose, a gym membership, massage classes.

Then she met Roger. He encouraged her to go to school and then on to a law degree, like his, only she, he said, could make hers into something. He paid her tuition, and this time with Roger's concern and appreciation as well as her own intelligence, Haley excelled at school. With the money she earned at the Golden Day, before their attempts at adult entertainment, she began paying Roger back, by giving him money, by getting herself close to a degree, and by allowing him to become the first man she truly, really cared for. She realized that helping her gave Roger pleasure. He had been too long without someone close to him. And the closer she got to him physically, the closer she got to him, becoming a part of his life, knocking away at shared concerns about living in his small, rented A-frame house out on Tram Road, on the verge of the piney woods, surrounded by pot growing neighbors. She filled his house with herself so that it became their house. Ironically, the closer she got to him within the house, within his life, the less she needed to physically rub up against him. And she felt it unfair that ultimately she would have to leave if she was going to ever get on with her life. He said, when the subject came up, that he understood.

"What's Roger said?" Barbara asked.

"I don't know," Haley said. "I haven't called him yet."

"You know you owe him that much," Barbara said.

"What do you owe a sugar daddy?" Dolores said.

Haley appreciated Barbara for glaring at Dolores and saying, "He is not just a sugar daddy. There's something there. Haley knows the difference. That's why she makes more money than you."

Because Barbara was beside her, Haley said, "We can sleep together."

"I bet you can," Dolores said.

"No, I mean that I can lay down with the man and literally sleep. He is there in that little house. And even when I don't try, I think about him."

"So you think he's going to be pissed?" Barbara asked.

"How can he not be," Dolores said.

"I've got to call him," Haley said. "He has to know." Then she caught herself, "Who are you going to call?"

"I was going to call your lawyer, Frank what's his name. But now I got nobody."

"Maybe Roger can help."

* * *

When Haley called to tell him that she was in jail on a prostitution charge, Roger went out the backdoor of his house to check on his dog. Harry was slobbering, moaning, and throwing himself against the gate of the picket fence that Roger had had built just for him. Harry could wag his tail and cry at the same time. He'd bark like a normal dog, but when he was happy and wanted someone to pay attention to him, he would moan. He craved attention more than food, so he moaned a lot. And what Harry wanted most was Roger petting him or just talking to him.

Roger pushed through the wall of humidity and heat and started sweating even before he got to Harry's gate. Roger reached over the gate to cradle Harry's jaw in his hand and then to rub his head. When Roger pulled his hand away, Harry raced around inside of his fence, wagging his tail. He was always happy, and though he liked everyone and would follow people, Harry preferred Roger. Roger's hand, with Harry's slobber on it, was now stinky too.

Harry was something of a freak. He had the short, stubby legs of a basset hound and the demeanor and head of a lab. From a distance, he looked like a furry, long-eared lab on his knees. He was fast, but his short legs made him clumsy. He was sort of like a slow torpedo. He had a thick chest and powerful hindquarters. With a head start, he would run to Roger and just throw himself at Roger, a couple of times knocking Roger over. When he found water, he scooted toward it like an amphibious landing craft. Roger once told Haley, "Harry's daddy was the guy who always said, 'I'll do her.'"

Besides the heartworm treatments, the shots, and the grooming, Roger paid for Harry's fence. Roger was not even sure that all the property that fence surrounded was what he rented. But the land gave Harry a shady, grassy playground. And Roger even had an awning stretched out from the house to give Harry a place to stay out of the rain and sun. When Roger let Harry out of his fence, his tongue lolling around outside his open mouth, no two feet hitting the ground in unison, Harry burrowed through the woods. Roger and Haley could track him by the shaking palms and tallow trees.

Harry had a habit of standing in front of a car to make it stop. And then, if the car was low enough and stopped, he would rest his front paws on the hood of the car, wag his tail, and moan. Out on Tram road, in the rain, Harry had stood in front of Haley's car and stopped her. She didn't know what to do with him, so she brought him home to Roger, as a joke and a gift. Roger named Harry after a man whom he had once spied upon, Harry Krammer. Krammer later got murdered. After two weeks with Harry, with Haley laughing at Harry, Roger just couldn't get rid of his dog.

Now, twice a day, Roger took Harry for a walk, and at five-thirty, when he went for his drinks at the Nothing To bar, right down Tram, even though he could have walked, he put Harry's leash on him, put him in the cab of the truck, and drove to the bar. Before he went in, Roger would park under a tree, put a large bowl of water in the bed of his pickup, and chain Harry to the bed. Even though Roger was his favorite, Harry had no attention span; he might desert Roger for anybody. The patrons and the owners of The Nothing Left to Lose Bar didn't like Harry because he stunk and, despite Roger's lessons at house training, couldn't be trusted not to pee inside. The reason why he went through the trouble that Harry demanded and what made Harry important to Roger was Haley.

As Roger turned his back to the moaning Harry and walked to his pickup, he finally felt something like heartburn making its way up from his chest. He kicked at the fender of his Toyota pickup. Maybe he had grown too old, too worn down, too burned out to respond to the fact that the woman living with him was involved in a prostitution ring. Maybe he was just neutered, like Harry. Maybe he had adopted Harry's demeanor. Maybe Harry had adopted his. He wondered, if at the jail, he would give just one long mournful moan like Harry's and then wag his tail and lick and nudge Haley when she came back to him.

In his truck driving through Beaumont, Roger rehearsed how he would talk and what he would say when he bailed Haley out of the new jail facility out on 69 near mid-county. The typical response was the redneck one: screaming, yelling, accusations. Or he could simply hug her. They could try a heart-to-heart talk with confessions and pleas for forgiveness.

But what plagued Roger was why Haley was soliciting men in the first place. Mid-evenings, after coming home from the Nothing to Lose, the beer and bourbon spreading throughout his body, and making him feel relaxed, Roger would make himself one more drink so that he felt a definite buzz. And he would wait for Haley to get home from school or work. This waiting, with just a touch of anticipation, was so much more pleasant than sitting at the Nothing to Lose as was his habit before meeting Haley. Roger would hear her pull up and then hear Harry moan, and she would come through the backdoor with a smile, and maybe some dinner, and they would kiss. Then after dinner, some TV, one last visit to Harry, then lying in bed, usually reading and chatting, rarely much sex since that was saved for special weekends or celebrations then drifting off to sleep and getting up early and getting started on another day of light work for him, heavy work and study for her, and then his routines: lunch, a long walk-and-jog, shower, Harry, bar, and so on. This was what he would have called, along with so many other people, boredom. But to Roger's surprise, since meeting Haley, he liked this boredom: the common, the ordinary, the mundane, the ritualistic ways we go spinning out our lives to fill up our time so as not to face any deep, annoying, ultimately destructive questions. Maybe, it was like Harry's life. Roger enjoyed his life with her because it was easy, so as he pulled into the new jail, he wondered if he should have been trying harder.

The jailers recognized him, for he often accompanied the bails bondsmen or visited clients or witnesses. As they let him into the halls that led to the cells, he thought that this was his world, not hers. He was the one with a life to hide, not her.

* * *

When they let her out of the holding tank and she walked down the hall to be released, Haley thought she could hear the snickers of the cops and jailers. When she got to the lobby, in front of her, in his shorts and t-shirt, grown shabbier and fatter since his knees started bothering him and he had to quit jogging, was her—her what: her lover, her partner, her live-in, her roommate—Roger Jackson. His experience, his nights hiding out and taking pictures of cheating spouses had sculpted his face into its latest form. His brows were furrowed. Wrinkles spread out from the outer corners of his eyes and did not go away when he stopped smiling. His chin had started to droop, and maybe, if he kept gaining weight, a double chin was not far away.

The moneyed-men she massaged spent a lot to arrest aging: tucks, pulls, gym memberships, massages, hell, her massages, the ones that got her arrested. But not Roger, he had surrendered to age or made truce with it or didn't notice it.

As she got closer to him, he opened his arms, and that gesture just sucked her right into him, and she wrapped her arms around him and pushed her head up under his chin and held him as tightly as she could.

Later that night, after dinner out, several drinks, happy hour at the Nothing To Lose Bar, they went through their usual rituals. They went out in the yard together, each with a drink, to feed Harry and to pet and pamper him one last time for the day, and they felt the slight drop in temperature and the rise in humidity that pressed in on Roger's A-Frame from out of the trees; and then after the TV nightly news and late shows, they climbed into bed, and Haley lay her head on Roger's chest to listen to his heart thump and waited for one or both of them to drift off to sleep. But neither one could sleep. "So do you want to talk about it?" Haley asked.

"I don't know what to say," Roger said.

Haley pulled her ear from Roger's chest, leaned to the other side of the bed and pushed the switch to the lamp. With both of them circled by the glow of the weak lamplight, Roger rolled over, away from Haley. "Eventually, we need to talk."

"I read somewhere that as a man gets older, rather than fight, he flees. Fighting could kill him. It could give him a heart attack."

"We're not fighting. We're talking."

"Right now, talking seems like fighting. You want to kill me?"

"Well, you're not sleeping."

"I'm thinking."

"So why don't you tell me what you are thinking."

"I'm not thinking very well."

Her arrest and humiliation had been performance. But once she had seen Roger, Haley had dropped all performance. In her mind, there was nothing to explain, she had simply been caught; now, perhaps, her plans might have to change. She could have gone to sleep with these facts, but seemingly, Roger could not. "This is nothing to be concerned about."

"Well, it does answer some things," Roger muttered.

"What does it answer?"

"We sleep. We just sleep. So you've found what you need with other people."

"What I needed was a financial arrangement."

"So you found my financial betters. You have your pick of moneyed people. And money buys time, and it buys looks. Hell, it buys right and wrong. So why wouldn't you be attracted to them? So no wonder you come home tired."

"Roger, why do you have to twist this like this."

"I know I'm older than you. I'm older than most people. I know I drink too much. I may not be what you're used to. Hell, I'm not what I'm used to."

"I don't like where you're taking this."

"So why are you even here?"

"I can do something with you, though, that I can't do with them."

"What's that?"

"Sleep."

There was a time when Haley would not have needed to explain at all. Instead, he said, "A person can sleep by himself."

Haley put her hand to her forehead to hold her thoughts in her forehead. "Excuse the cliché,, but I'm not just fucking with you."

"No, you're not fucking with me at all. You're fucking them."

"Roger, don't. Please don't. Don't be the smart-assed you. Smart-ass you can be cruel."

"You mean don't be me."

"Roger, Roger. Oh God. Be you. But don't be mean. You aren't mean. You don't mean to be mean. So don't."

"So you're telling me, I have no cause to be mean to you? Couldn't I try being mean just a little to see if that helps?"

"So then go ahead and be mean."

"I don't feel like it any more."

Despite her grades, despite her skill in writing, she could not make the right sentences for Roger. The more she tried, the more his quick responses confused her. So Haley squeezed her forehead so tightly that she was sure she left pink fingerprints. She muzzled herself and rolled on her side away from Roger because she feared that if either of them said anymore, the other would start yelling. She waited for two hours before she heard Roger snoring.

* * *

Afterwards, for several months, they settled into a quiet truce with only occasional bouts of Roger's frustration, when Roger, not knowing what else to do, would make the first smart-assed comment that would come to his mind. What he wanted to do was yell. When he got frustrated, Haley could tell and would leave him to himself in his cabin while she went out for a drink or ice cream or a burger. And Roger would sit by himself and wonder why he had to say anything at all. He didn't mean what he said to her; the smart-assing was just something to do. So instead of relaxing, they were just quiet. They slept warily together.

So they discussed the weather, homework, TV shows. Sex was completely gone. They could have confused themselves for a tolerant but estranged father and daughter. Partially, they were waiting for Haley's trial.

The trial wasn't a problem. They didn't even need that good of a lawyer. For, in Texas, cops were indiscriminate about prostitution charges, and defense attorneys and judges knew it. So while Haley was convicted, her sentence was light: the crime classified as a misdemeanor so she wouldn't have a life penalized with a felony. She got a $1500 fine, and no jail time. So she returned to Roger. On a January night, with the rain falling through the trees to plink on the tin roof and with Harry moaning at intervals because he wanted inside for a treat and a few minutes lying at Roger's feet, Haley told Roger that she was going to prove to him why they should be thankful for each other.

Haley made Roger stretch out naked the length of a long portable, folding table set up in the kitchen. His toes stretched out over the edge, and he rested his head on his folded arms. "Look at me," she said. Roger rolled his head to the side in the direction of Haley's voice and squinted through the red haze of their dining room. Haley had replaced the three regular light bulbs with muted, low-wattage red ones, she had filled the room with sticks of old incense that gave off a cinnamon smell but left little clouds of smoke wafting around the dining room. When he located her in the dark, Haley pulled one then the other bow holding her shoulder to thigh length terry cloth shift in place, wriggled, and then straightened as the shift settled around her feet. She was completely naked, not even make up, no paint on her finger or toe nails. "Look at me," Haley told him.

"I'm looking," Roger said.

"Look longer. Study me." Roger looked and noted that she had captured her own specific beauty.

"Now roll back over," Haley told Roger.

He did as he was told to peer over the edge of the table at his dirty floor. Then he felt Haley's greased elbows poking into his shoulders. He grunted and looked back over his shoulder at her. He saw just her face, straining but concentrating, just above his ear, as she pushed her weight on to her elbows. "Turn back around," she commanded. Roger did as he was told. "Look at me." Roger felt what must have been a drop of her warm sweat splatter on his back. She was working hard. "Now, turn over again."

Roger turned around, then felt the points of her elbows work slowly from his shoulders to his mid-back, then to his butt. The hurt turned soothing. And he felt his muscles stop resisting so that he felt the pressure down beneath his muscles and into his organs. He grunted. Then the pressure was gone. He missed it. So he turned his head to see Haley, through the red haze, rubbing oil all over her naked body. She slowly stepped to him, then took his head in her hands, turned it back so that he was looking at the floor, and straddled him. Then the tips of her thumbs began to work their way through the same territory softened by her elbows. She must have been trying to show him what she gave to her customers. He liked it.

By the time she started digging into Roger's back with the heels of her palms, the pressure had lost all pain. Roger turned into a puddle. Then Haley rubbed with her flat palms, and Roger lost track of time, calculating it only by Harry's intermittent moans. She stepped off of him again. Then she rubbed a lotion on him that felt like peppermint tasted, and then she piled smooth rocks heated in the oven over the length of his body. Slowly, she picked each rock off his back.

Now a sizzling puddle, Roger moaned with pleasure. Then she rolled him over so that he was back-down on the table, then straddled him again, this time just with her hips and thighs, guiding him into her. And she didn't move so much as undulate, contract and compress her every organ. More than aroused, Harry felt alive.

Then with the sweat and oil on both them, she slid from off of him and lay on top of him, writhing, only internally, through the contractions of muscles. Within a few moments, she started to cry. And then Roger quietly cried. Harry moaned.

For awhile they lay on each other, an exhausted puddle that had once been two distinct puddles. And when Roger got some presence of mind, he saw a clock. This had taken an hour and half. Since he was aware, Roger stepped off of the table, walked through the kitchen, opened the door, and let Harry in. Some of the cloud of humidity, cold, and rain followed Harry in to mix with the warm, the red, sweat and lotion filled haze. "What the hell," Roger said to Haley and shrugged.

Harry charged through the house dripping and banging into furniture like a malfunctioning, clumsy torpedo. Haley chuckled, "he stinks." She started laughing. "So I just give you the best massage I'm capable of and you let him in. What are you thinking?"

Naked Roger sat in his recliner in his living room and now yelled at Harry. Harry curled, as best the fat, long dog could, at Roger's feet. Oily, shivering Haley stepped in front of Roger and laughed uncontrollably. He stared at naked, laughing Haley. She stared back at his nakedness and hugged herself to make herself stop laughing. "What do you feel now?"

"Disorientation, confusion . . . ecstasy."

"I feel the same way."

Roger rose from his recliner and stepped toward her. Harry twisted to look a the two of them. "I could give my clients only half of that. And I couldn't let Harry in afterwards." Roger felt drained. "It was a performance for them, Roger."

"It was still fucking them," Roger said, but he didn't mean that to be a mean comment.

"That was all I did. But look at what we can do. Why have we wasted a minute of our time? Eventually I'll leave because I'll just run out of what I can do here. We've always known that. But until then . . . "

In the red light, Roger could see Haley pleading with her eyes. A person was lucky to find an hour and half like he had just had. Then Roger felt Harry's rough tongue gently scrape up his ankle. Without Harry, without this A-Frame on the edge of the woods, without the pot growing neighbors and the broken down bar, The Nothing To Lose, that hour wouldn't be possible and wouldn't be repeatable. He had been lucky and yet he had worked at this luck too. What he hadn't been was aware of what he had stumbled upon and what he had done to keep it and how it was temporary and fragile. And here he had been squandering time when he should have been aware of it.

"What do you say, Roger?" Haley asked.

Roger, after being away from himself too long, came back to himself, "If Harry weren't so long, he'd be able to lick his own ass. That's one of a dog's biggest pleasures. It's what makes a dog a dog. He ought to be miserable. But look at him. You think he minds?"

Haley took a tentative step toward him. Harry ran through the house, banging into the furniture.

"And you gave him to me," Roger said. Then he looked at naked, oily Haley. "I no longer mind," he said.

Contrabandista Epistle

Dear Marilyn:

    I guess I should be ashamed to admit to my ex-wife that I like to take hot baths with whores, but after all, I run Cleburne Hot Springs Resorts, and the whores are good company, and they deliver. So anymore, I call up one of the whorehouses from la zona over in Ojinaga, and they drive over, usually in some big old aircraft-looking American car you see only in Mexico anymore.

    Cleburne Hot Springs bubble under the main cabin, which is mine. My uncle put a pipe from that 110-degree water right up into this big old bathtub built into the floor in the middle of the main suite (my stucco cabin) of Cleburne Hot Springs Resort. My family's resort has another pipe gushing out hot water in the bathhouse that has three of its own baths. And the drainage follows the wash on down to the Rio Grande and makes a nice, but hot creek running through the middle of my resort.

    A few nights back, I had a surprise party for Dolph, my roommate. My cabin was dark and cold, but warming from the vapors of steam from the hot water in my tub. Candles around the tub lit the place and gave it dancing shadows. I was sipping a beer, watching my belly float in the hot water, and spitting my snuff into the beer can with the top carved off with my army can opener. (Yes, I still do that "disgusting" habit, but what should whores care?) Water dripped from the two twisted ends of my moustache, and the older whore had my ear lobe in between her index finger and thumb to look at the diamond stud earring I have put there since you left me. She looked at it like she planned to steal it or put it in her own ear.

    So, Dolph walks on in, and because he is dressed in his Border Patrol uniform, the younger whore gets spooked, and whispers, "la migra."

    "La patrulla," Dolph, who can get touchy about the Border Patrol, said. The folks in Presidio like the Border Patrol. Border Patrol Agents are well paid compared to most of the dirt-poor residents and drop a lot of money and help on the town. So the Presidio Mexicans call them la patrulla, not la migra.

The older whore, who is my favorite, let go of my diamond stud earring and slapped at her colleague and giggled. "Su compañero," she said.

"You, Dolph, peel off them clothes and jump in," I said. "You know Alice Kramden here," I said and pointed to the older whore. "And this is Wilma Flintstone."

Alice Kramden leaned back against the edge of the tub and reached for a pack of cigarettes. She nonchalantly lit one up and said "Hola, pretty boy" to Dolph. And since she was smoking, I spit some of my snuff juice into my sliced beer can.

"Jump in, pretty boy," I said.

"Go to hell," Dolph said. Mexican women, even his own mother, have called Dolph pretty boy all his life. But it pisses Dolph off cause he's as old as me. Though in a lot ways, he gets these dreamy kind of moods like a kid gets, especially lately, since he thinks he is in love with this tall Viking-looking woman who runs the hotel at Walter Landers' goddamn Disneyland over in Lajitas.

Dolph unbuckled his holster and held it away from him like it was a rattler, then walked to the king-sized bed, and dropped the belt and holster on the pillows. Then he slipped out of his uniform, shivered a little, and stared at what was floating: the two whores' titties and my gut.

"Cogelo ese," the older whore said to the younger one, and the girl swished across the large tub to Dolph and rubbed his back, then actually kissed the goddamn scar on his belly where he was shot all to hell by a kid smuggling marijuana and was dragged to safety by Sister Quinn. The older whore wrapped her arms around me and pulled me closer to her, and the hot water steamed off us, and some dripped from her nose into her large, sagging cleavage. Of course, she could never replace you, Marilyn, but she is a damn sight better than wife number two, and less demanding than wife number three.

"Cómo te llama?" Dolph politely asked the young whore. Dolph had been to Border Patrol sensitivity training sessions up in El Paso, started because American-Mexicans were complaining, not that Dolph ever needed any refining. Marilyn, Dolph is probably more of what you told me you wanted me to be.

"Wilma Flintstone," the young whore said.

"Alice Kramden," my whore said and jerked her thumb toward her chest.

I tossed Dolph a beer, then leaned into the arm that Alice Kramden had around my shoulders. She reached around to the side of my head and twisted the end of my wet moustache.

My other roommate, you remember him, ol' Ignacio, had given Dolph some chili, which is mostly what we eat, and told him we were in the tub.

Ignacio is pretty much worthless anymore, just too old. But he half-assed raised me, taught me riding and Spanish. And now I kind of raise him. I pay for his dental bills. I'd even pay for a doctor if he'd ever go. And at Christmas, we exchange Christmas cards. He claims he's a Catholic—though I've never seen him go to a church—so he doesn't cavort with whores, would rather watch one of the TV sets I gave him.

So Dolph starts in on me (just like you did after the divorce, when we would get to talking too long on the phone): "Ignacio is throwing rocks into your pool again. Says he wants to fill it up."

Dolph gave me one of his pissy looks as Wilma Flintstone started running a finger down his chest and then his scar.

"Listen, I tear up that piece of shit pool I got and put in this fiber-glass thing."

"Where you going to get the money?"

"My relatives."

"Pepper, who is going to drive to the middle of nowhere to go to hot springs in a desert?"

"That's why I need the pool and the bar."

"Why don't you leave this place as it is and rent to the few people who know about it?"

"Because those fuckers in Lajitas with the fake looking Western town bullshit motif did a million worth of business last year. I wish I had a beer drinking goat like Ronnie Lewis' goddamn Clay Henry down at Lajitas."

"They're also located next to a national park with just a few cabins for lodging."

"Ojinaga has a park." I looked at Wilma then Alice, "if I could just peddle gambling and prostitutes, I'd have the best resort in Texas."

Later that night, after everybody was asleep, I felt like staggering outside, like I did sometimes late at night when Dolph would start to get to me, and piss in my leaking pool. Hell Marilyn, that goddamn Houston sue-crazy lawyer, Walter Landers, came out to Big Bend Park and saw Ronnie Lewis's falling down, worthless trading post at Lajitas; fed beers to that goddamn Clay Henry, that beer guzzling goat, the mayor of Lajitas; watched Mexicans rowing across the river; and dreamed up a resort. Ronnie's granddaddy started Lajitas, same as my granddaddy started the whole goddamn cattle business in the Trans-Pecos. And all Lajitas was was a trading post that the Coahuila and Chihuahua Mexicans brought their sotol, candelilla, and furs to for sixty years. And now dope smuggling has all but killed the illegal candelilla and sotol smuggling to this country. And then Walter Landers buys the land around the trading post from Ronnie and turns it into fucking Disneyland nine hole golf course, first a couple of motel rooms, then a hotel, then a bar, then a pool. I've got the hot springs for winter, all I need is that pool, and the tourists will drive their Winnebagos through the gate of my uncle's old ranch property and then honk their horns until I come running out and assign them a camping spot or a cabin.

My uncle built the cabins in the thirties and had a pretty good business. I've added the entertainment complex. The kitchen has silver metal, industrial strength refrigerators and stoves and tables. I got them from a Holiday Inn up in Pecos that went broke. Outside its swinging doors is the dining room with round wooden, fake Western tables and chairs. And to the left is a long bar with a brass rail from a bar that went broke up in Odessa. I got a silver artisan in Chihuahua to hammer me out some copper fittings for the corner of my bar. In the game room, from that same gone-broke Holiday Inn, are lamps with Western figures—cowboys, Indians, cattle—all lighting a pool table (from a friend of a friend in Ojinaga) and a foosball table from Sul Ross up in Alpine.

So I got entertainment, relaxation, and hot water, but I need that pool, but this goddamn shifting desert sand keeps cracking it, like this goddamn desert is going to suck ever last drop of water back into its core, even if that water is near boiling hot.

But my pool is no longer my biggest problem. Marilyn, I've fucked

up. It is what I wanted to tell you, but now I can't write it down. What I really want is to see you again. To see my son just once more. Couldn't you fly as far as Odessa, I'd pick you up? Couldn't you send Trey to see me? Always yours,
Pepper Cleburne

* * *

Dear Marilyn:

My hands didn't start shaking the bourbon out of my glass when you left. That started when the third Mrs. Cleburne left me for that smooth, Yankee real estate developer in Alpine, with his promotions of "rustic cabins" on Davis Mountains lots, "the real old west." The second Mrs. Cleburne isn't worth talking about. No, when you left, I lost my business sense.

When you and Trey left, I rented a small house to a cowboy and his family from Wyoming and let them do most of the repairing and herding. I gave Ignacio a bedroom and let him watch for torn fences, coyotes, or loose cattle. I let the business end go. All I did, since I could still keep my bourbon in my glass, was to sit on our (then my, now *my* cousin *Harold's*) back porch and look at some of the prettiest high desert grazing land in the country.

When my granddaddy drove his cattle west from south Texas, bound for Arizona, a place he'd never seen, at least his eyes and instincts didn't fail him so he just stopped at the edge of the Davis Mountains. Good grass, cool climate (for Texas), level pastures with natural boundaries. The problem with granddaddy is, that once he decided to get married, well into his forties, he just couldn't stop having kids, and then those kids started having kids. It's like my family just doesn't know what causes the bastards. And now ranching has become a rich man's hobby. Maybe my uncle, the black sheep back then, who ignored his cattle and built these stucco cabins back in the 30s, could see all this coming. He was a visionary like me.

When my hands started shaking my bourbon out of my glass because the third Mrs. Pepper Cleburne left me, I decided to give up *the* ranch (used to *our* ranch, never feeling it was *my* ranch), for education. And I figured I'd be satisfied with books and give up on women. Like I always say, and like you always cuss me for saying, "if it wasn't for that furry spot between their legs, there'd be a bounty on them." I got what I needed: an apartment in Alpine, my son for a roommate, and an interest in books. As Trey started to high school and I started college at Sul Ross, I think we straightened each other out. The Mexicans and the cowboys in Alpine were good for Trey, and I'd like to think I was too. Leastwise, I believe I sent him back to you in better shape than when I got him.

Maybe the happiest time was after that when I was teaching practically everything out in Valentine, Texas. The students were good because their ranching daddies or wetback parents told them that they didn't have no choice but to do good in school. But then, my family had no one to tend Cleburne Hot Springs, and being the black sheep, and owing uncles and cousins money, I drove down off the south rim, dropped out of the high grazing land and into the low desert, and became the manager of Cleburne Hot Springs Resorts. (I substitute now in Presidio, and the kids know my car and face and will yell out at me, "Yo, Pepper." And I have found that, like in Valentine, teachers can party a whole lot.)

The first thing I did as manager was to build my entertainment complex and then, with Ignacio searching through his dim memory for his mama's recipe, made the chili that took second place in the Terlingua World Champion Chili Cook-Off. We eat chili a lot now, because Ignacio and I have sworn that we're eventually going to win the Terlingua World Chili Championship. Then I started building my pool. I got some Mexicans to sneak across at Candelaria (lying bastards said they had built pools at resorts in the interior), borrowed a bulldozer from the highway department, read some books about swimming pools, and with them and Ignacio, I built this goddamn leaking swimming pool.

My point starts ten days ago this morning. I loaded Ignacio into my orange and white Chevy to drive out to see my business partner. Yes Marilyn, I still have the Chevy. The kids all know it. Only in Mexico can I get the parts, paint, upholstery, and labor to keep it up. Mexicans don't have computers yet. So maybe it's good that I'm now closer to Mexico.

Vincent Fuentes, my partner, had called me and told me to meet him in Paso Lajitas. In Mexico are ejidos that are official, government sponsored projects, and unofficial, the ones close to some American settlement where peons can hope to live off what Americans throw away. Paso Lajitas folks try to live off Wally Landers' Disneyland in Lajitas.

Lajitas is the last pass on the river before the big canyons in Big Bend. The flagstone on the river bottom made it an easy place to cross. Which is why Ronnie Lewis' great grandfather put his trading post here, and thus, why Walter Landers saw Ronnie's beer drinking goat and made his own Disneyland.

In Paso Lajitas is an open-air restaurant and one bar. Inside the bar are Playboy centerfolds and a big sign that translates to something like, "you owe money, I own your ass." And under the sign is a list of names of people who needed to pay up.

In this bar are restrooms just like in America, but once you step through the right door, you are outside. Farther along is an adobe wall separating the sexes, and just at the end of the wall is a cliff. The custom is to piss off the edge of the cliff and then throw your beer can over the edge. So there's this pile of cans working its way up the cliff. And just beyond the beer cans is a goatherder's shack.

The goatherder's name is Pepe. Before Fuentes and I met him he sold kids to restaurants and grocery stores for cabrito. That day, he was sitting out by the river with a bamboo fishing pole dangling a line into the river, and his wife was hanging up laundry.

I left Ignacio in the bar, walked around the beer cans baking in the piss and sun, and waved to Pepe. He motioned for me to go in. I made my way through the goats standing in front of Pepe's jacal, around the blowing laundry, past his wife. I knocked.

"Quien es?" I heard

"Un amigo de la hermana," I answered.

The door slowly opened, and I saw Sister Quinn in the doorway. Sister Quinn smiled and moved to one side so that I could step into the room. As I stepped around her, she closed and locked the door behind me. Sister Quinn looks like a stack of tires, the Michelin nun. And as usual, she had a tennis hat shoved down on her head, pasting her red Irish curls to her forehead.

My boot heels tapped against the plyboards that Pepe had trimmed to make himself a floor. Sunlight spilled in through cracks in the walls and splits in the tin roof.

Vincent Fuentes was wearing khaki pants and a white t-shirt, and he sat in a wooden folding chair at a small table. Behind the table was a window with a view of the Lajitas crossing and a little farther on and above the start of El Camino del Rio, Texas 170. On the table, was a half-empty bottle of tequila, a small white mound of powder, binoculars, and a cordless phone. Fuentes bought Pepe the binoculars and the phone, so he could watch the river and call Fuentes when it was clear, high, or low. Fuentes sent out drivers in new Broncos or Suburbans, just like American or Mexican families, and they drove across, or he sent across mules ,and they hiked inland over some of the roughest country in the state, through the new state park, just like backpackers, until Sister Quinn or I could pick them up and drive them and their goods to Alemán in Pecos.

Fuentes and I didn't try the crossings at the International Bridge in Presidio, and la plaza and some meaner, bigger Americans ran their goods across around Candelaria. We couldn't afford a plane. So we pretended to be tourists. We figured that tourists wouldn't want to see drug busts right next to their camping grounds.

I turned to Sister Quinn, "I didn't see that truck you drive. How did you get here?"

"I flew," she said but did not giggle. The locals call Sister Quinn a curandera, and they say she can turn into an owl and fly around at nights and perch on tombstones. She's my other business partner.

"Sister Quinn, Ignacio is in the tejano bar. How about you joining him and telling him we'll be here a while?" Fuentes looked at her and nodded his head.

When she got all of her body out of the shack, Fuentes and I both groaned. Fuentes' hair was dabbled with grey, and he had a cowlick in front. The muscles in his face drooped, and the bags up under his eyes held his bloodshot eyes in his head. "Whether she flew or not, she's still crazy," he said.

I pulled a metal folding chair up to the table and sat down. Fuentes smiled, leaned across the table, and said, "You may have either or both." He looked at the cocaine and the tequila bottle.

"You're kidding," I said.

"I've developed a few habits." He reached across the table, but didn't grab the liquor or the dope, but instead brought back a pair of round eyeglasses. He put them on and looked like a professor. He squinted at me;

his head started to circle.

"It's early in the morning yet. How long you been drinking?" I asked.

"For years," he said.

He dropped his head into his hands, "I'm thinking about walking across the river and turning myself in. I want to be prosecuted in America." I could smell the liquor on his breath.

"Mexican taxpayers ought to pay to prosecute their own dope dealers."

He shook his head like he was real sorry. "Most of my bad habits started because I was in a Mexican jail."

"I'm not sure I want you arrested anywhere."

He exhaled, "You think Sister Quinn could choose not to be crazy? There is no real choice; this little thing happens, then this one, and you put them together . . ." He rested his elbows on the table and looked across at me. He tried again, "The people we work with had a misunderstanding." He shrugged, "One side now cooperates with la plaza. La plaza works with the local army garrison in Ojinaga by reporting little contrabandistas. All of them would like to see me dead."

"Holy shit. So we're out of business?"

He nodded, "In a jail in the U.S., I'm a wealth of information. I can help fight the war on drugs.'"

"If you eat with the devil, you better use a long spoon."

He smiled at me and then frowned and pushed up the cowlick in front of his head. "We all have short spoons."

I should have shot him. Nobody in Pasa Lajitas would have stopped me. Bad for business. I could have packed up Sister Quinn and Ignacio, driven back to my resort, and finished my pool.

Instead, Ignacio and I drove Sister Quinn back to her templo. She sat in the back seat jabbering as she always does about the plight of the dark-skinned in a white world, the suffering of the poor, the misery of being human. I was pretty goddamn miserable myself, and Ignacio raised his hands to his ears to signal her to shut the hell up.

Sister Quinn's templo is in Redford, where the land flattens out; the poor locals, first Indians, then Mexicans, have been farming there for centuries. Beyond an onion field (Presidio grows the best by-god onions in Texas), and right before the salt-cedars start advancing down to the river is Sister Quinn's templo. The locals got together and built up the old shack and then built a hut next to it for her quarters. When she got out of my Chevy, as fat as she was, Sister Quinn made a beeline for the templo. Ignacio reached into the glove compartment and pulled out the manila envelop and handed it to me. We got out and followed her to the door of the templo while she fiddled with a key to unlock the padlock on the door. When she got the door open, sunlight rolled into her weird church and she followed it to the altar. She smiled at us, thanked us, then knelt under the wooden statues of Jesus and the Virgin.

At the back of the templo, like he was watching her with his old cataract-covered eyes, his white handkerchief, which he used for his cures on his knees, was a photo of the old 19th century curandero Pedrito Jarmillo. The donation box was in front of Pedrito's photo. I dropped the envelope in the box.

Sister Quinn thought she was smuggling political refugees from Central America into the country, thought she was helping the poor of the world to become richer poor in this country, so she wouldn't take any money for doing the Lord's or ol' Pedrito Jarmillo's work. So I dropped five hundred dollars at a time in her collection box. I had bought most of the ornaments in her church.

Marilyn, it all started with refrigerators. You see, Mexicans tax the hell out of everything not homegrown, especially anything American. So I met a guy in Ojinaga who knew some people in Chihuahua City and on down in Puebla who were in the unauthorized appliance business, so I started buying refrigerators and hiding them from Dolph in the vacant cabins or out in some of the old line shacks left over from when my family was still trying to run cattle in this desert.

Pretty soon, my guy introduces me to Vincent Fuentes. He's an ex-priest, ex-professor, ex-prominent member of the P.R.I. I mean he is the best Mexico has to offer. And as a result, he knows how everything works. He had a real sob story: these peons in Zacetecas and then these urban guerrillas needed guns to defend themselves from the army. I had a federal permit to buy semi-automatic weapons, so I'd buy them, ship them over to him, and make three times what I'd paid for them. Hell, you ever try to swim across a river with a refrigerator, guns are a lot lighter. Then instead of cash we got paid in drugs, I mean real drugs. I had rhino horn to give oriental guys hard-ons, designer drugs, illegal cancer "cures," aphrodisiacs, amphetamines, Quaaludes, and anything else that the F.D.A. didn't approve but could be shipped through Mexico. So Fuentes would arrange to get the drugs across, and then I had to sell them. So I found "Al,man" in Pecos, and he gave me four times what I could make with guns. It was too much; I had the money, but I couldn't even use it to fix that goddamn pool or renovate my cabins for fear of giving myself away. I should have stuck to refrigerators.

Could you come see me? Write? Call?

Love,

Pepper

* * *

Dear Marilyn:

Fuentes set up one more shipment with a bunch of mules back-paking across the desert and into the high canyons. He sent Sister Quinn to pick them up, and then he probably phoned the Border Patrol himself.

On a cold night, when the desert actually got some snow, Dolph commanded an ambush of those mules and caught them and Sister Quinn. But Dolph's a sharp fella and listens close to the local talk. He probably had everything figured out before Fuentes could make it to this side of the river and trade my name for a deal. Once Dolph knew, he had to turn me in. He thinks himself to be above la mordida, but he stills takes baths with my whores.

He did the decent thing, though, and drove out to a gate Ignacio was repairing and told Ignacio to clear out. Ignacio was too old to do any jail time, and as far as any of us knew, Ignacio had relatives in Mexico and nobody in la plaza or the army gave much of a shit about him. Then Ignacio told me what was coming. And then, not going to his cabin, but heading out into the desert, Ignacio disappeared.

The next day, I was up early, as usual (I don't sleep much anymore, Marilyn), and Cleburne Hot Springs Resort was under invasion by the Customs Office, the Border Patrol, the D.E.A., and the Presidio County Sheriff's Department. After they gave me a warrant, officers in and out of uniform were tearing up my cabin, cutting the velvet on my pool table, going through my pots and pans. Because most of the arresting agents knew me, because they knew I had no backdoor, rather than making me sit in my own dining room handcuffed to a chair, they let me go into the kitchen and cook up some chili. I took off my boots, sliced off the top of a beer can, shoved some Beechnut in my bottom lip, and started slicing Presidio onions for my chili.

Dolph didn't bother tearing up the resort. He drove a motorcycle through desert washes until he found the old-line shack with refrigerators, semi-automatics, and pharmaceuticals. When he came into my kitchen to talk to me before they busted me, he was pretty pissed off because his own people had spread his stuff all over the ground.

Dolph pushed open the swinging door to the kitchen, just as the smell of my chili was filling the room. I had my boots off and my spit can on the table next to my beer. So I sat down to enjoy what time I had left with my vices. (I wish I had called the whores the night before and asked them to stay for breakfast.) "Why you cooking the chili?" Dolph asked.

"Thought these boys might need some lunch," I said and let some juice dribble into my can. "Probably the best chili they'll ever get. You want a beer?"

"I'm on-duty, but I'm talking to you off-duty."

I can't remember or make up what Dolph said other than "Aw shit, Pepper." Mainly he asked me all the whys, whats, and wherefores I just told you. I do remember that we couldn't look at each other, and I took my earring out and handed it to him for his safekeeping. In a way, I felt as sorry for him as for me, not because he was busting his best buddy and landlord, but because way down inside he understood why I did what I did but was not about to admit to himself that he understood. Dolph was just starting to admit things to himself.

Just as we got to a point where we could look at each other and tried to say something that there was no reason nor way to say, the kitchen filled with all brands and varieties of cops. I stuck my hands in front of me and asked, "Can we do this front ways?"

Somebody whispered, "Sorry," when I got the cuffs on.

"You fellas help yourself to that chili. I made it for y'all," I said as they led me out of the kitchen.

I took one last look at my entertainment room. Then outside, I stopped, making all the law enforcement officers stop with me, and we all looked at my piss-poor pool. "Take care of that goddamn pool for me, will you, Dolph?"

"Fuck that pool," Dolph said.

Then, I saw some guys in navy blue windbreakers with D.E.A. printed on the back leading a handcuffed Ignacio. They put me and Ignacio into the same Border Patrol truck and drove us to Marfa. That fool Mexican should have cleared out to his Mexico relations.

Always my love,

Pepper

* * *

Dear Marilyn:

Vincent Fuentes is probably dead now; nobody tells me much. Sister Quinn got arrested, but the law figured out she was crazy, that she did believe she was helping political refugees. She's got a pretty good insanity plea. The church wants to excommunicate her. Guess Ignacio and I are pretty lucky. Dolph and an uncle in Alpine got together bail money for the both of us, and my uncle hired a lawyer from San Antonio.

I am now confined to my uncle's ranch while I wait for a trial, and Dolph is taking care of my resort. I mostly sit out under what little shade there is in my uncle's backyard, sip a beer, and stare off at the South Rim. On a clear day, I can see across the desert at the north side of the Chinatis. Those flattened peaks change from orange to blue to pink. And on the other side of them is Cleburne Hot Springs Resort. Dolph is probably sitting under what little shade there is at Cleburne Hot Springs and staring at the south side of the Chinatis. Sometimes he calls me and tells me about his troubles with romance. I'll ask him if he me wants to call my Ojinaga whores, so far he refuses (I think his hand is shaking the bourbon out of his glass). From staring out into the desert looking for dope and wetbacks, Dolph can point out a moving puff of dust in the desert and can tell just how fast somebody is driving, and he wonders, when he spots the dust off-duty, if some smuggler is driving fast over back ranch roads.

No view is like the one from the back porch of our house. I like to remember that—almost like in the movie Giant—I brought this sophisticated Dallas lady home to a ranch in Trans-Pecos Texas. You could say that my Liz Taylor grew restless and bored on the ranch and begin taking pills with her liquor and that I further developed my taste in rough looking West Texas waitresses. And now you got your own life, and our son has his. But I remember that maybe it was y'all that made me want to fix that goddamn pool in the first place.

If you want, come out. Send Trey out. There's nothing in the law that says you can't see me.

Love, please,

Pepper